Keely, **Emma** and **Tahlia** work together
at a small, trendy design company in Melbourne.
They've become the best of friends, meeting for
breakfast, chatting over a mid-morning coffee
and a doughnut—or going for a cocktail after work.
They've loved being single in the city…but now
three gorgeous new men are about to enter their work
lives, transform their love lives—and give them
loads more to gossip about!

Don't miss each story in this great new trilogy
brought to you by Mills & Boon® Tender Romance™!

Office Gossip
*From sexy bosses to surprise babies—
these girls have got everyone talking!*

September 2005:
Impossibly Pregnant by Nicola Marsh

Last month, October 2005:
The Shock Engagement by Ally Blake

This month, November 2005:
Taking on the Boss by Darcy Maguire

Darcy Maguire spends her days as a matchmaker, torturing tall, handsome men, seducing them into believing in love, and romancing their socks off! And when she's not working on her novels she enjoys gardening, reading and going to the movies. She loves to hear from readers. Visit her at www.darcymaguire.com

Recent titles by the same author:

THE BRIDAL CHASE
THE FIANCÉE CHARADE
A CONVENIENT GROOM*
THE BEST MAN'S BABY*
A PROFESSIONAL ENGAGEMENT*

*The Bridal Business trilogy

TAKING ON
THE BOSS

BY
DARCY MAGUIRE

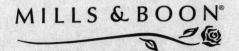

MILLS & BOON®

First published in Great Britain 2005
Harlequin Mills & Boon Limited,
Eton House, 18-24 Paradise Road, Richmond, Surrey TW9 1SR

© Debra D'Arcy 2005

ISBN 0 263 84270 3

Set in Times Roman 10½ on 12½ pt.
02-1105-40454

Printed and bound in Spain
by Litografía Rosés, S.A., Barcelona

CHAPTER ONE

Aries—Your love life has been in a lull. Expect to meet someone new who'll stir your passions.
No, thank you, I'll pass.

'It's every girl's dilemma.'

Tahlia Moran pushed open the front door to their office building, turning and holding it for her friend. 'What is?'

'The right timing to get seriously into finding one's life's partner, of course,' Keely said, pushing her handbag strap up her shoulder.

The words hammered right through Tahlia. First the horror-scope and now Keely. Did she have 'seriously single but feel free to cure me' tattooed on her forehead?

'You know,' Keely offered. 'It has to be soon or there won't be any single, straight men left for you. All the good men are getting snapped up.'

Tahlia had to admit her two best friends were doing their bit, going from seriously single to seriously taken in what seemed like a snap. 'I'm fine. I don't need anybody just now.'

'Tahlia—' Keely moved slowly through the doorway, resting her arm on her protruding belly, full of arms and legs. 'I know a lot of women just wait for him to appear, like magic. But we do encourage him

5

to turn up by dating, pitiful though it may be, every single man around.'

'Just in case he doesn't,' Tahlia stated dryly, glancing down at her friend, who was a good six inches shorter than her now that Keely had traded in her heels for flats that didn't add to the swelling she seemed to be experiencing in more places than just her belly.

'Mr Right turned up for me and Em. He will for you too, but you have to date. It's a given, an unwritten agreement with Cupid.'

Tahlia let the door go. 'I'm thrilled for you both, you know that, but I have things to do right now and those things have nothing to do with arrow-wielding midgets or men.' While a partner was on her to-do list he wasn't a priority just now. And when it came to relationships she was in uncharted territory—a place she'd rather not be.

Keely sighed. 'Okay, but he *could* just appear out of nowhere and sweep you off your feet.'

She didn't want to be swept; she was thinking more of being quietly and calmly romanced into a sane and sensible partnership that would prove companionable and satisfying for the long term, some time in the future.

'What does your horoscope say?'

Tahlia tucked her bag tightly under her arm. She'd had quite enough of horoscopes. It wasn't as if they were always right. In fact, they were hardly right at all…so it didn't really matter what it said today.

'Oh, look, there's George.' Tahlia veered towards the guard's desk, sneaking a quick glance at her friend to see if she'd successfully avoided discussing her horror-scope and its nebulous prediction of a certain stirring someone entering her life. 'I've got to thank him for letting me out last night.'

Keely continued across the large marbled foyer towards the lifts. 'Locked in again, eh?'

Tahlia nodded, straightening her suit jacket. There was only one way to guarantee being the only choice for the position of Marketing Executive and that was to out-work and out-perform everyone else.

There was no doubt she'd get the position when the big boss, Raquel, stopped running around the place trying to tell everyone how to do their jobs, and do hers by finally filling the position.

Tahlia couldn't help but smile. Raquel's job would be so much easier once she gave Tahlia the promotion, if only Raquel would get over her fear that Tahlia wanted her job next, rational or not.

'You know, you've got to get out there to find him,' her friend called across the foyer.

Tahlia stared after her, shaking her head and glancing around her. Trust Keely to share her singledom with the world.

She was well aware of the fact that she wasn't just going to bump into the perfect man, that she had to go out and find him, eventually, but there were so many more pressing things to deal with first.

First and foremost, she had to secure that promotion. She needed to have job security before mucking around in the dating scene and possibly finding a partner, just in case it didn't work out.

She wasn't going to go into any relationship blind,

unprepared, naïvely optimistic, or with silly ideas like love was enough.

Her mum had put her career on hold while she had concentrated on motherhood. When things had come crashing down her mother had been left juggling it all, finding out just how hard life was if you neglected sense and relied on love to see you through.

Tahlia was going to wait.

She wasn't going to be pressured into something she wasn't ready for just because Emma and Keely were no longer single. She'd wait until after the announcement of her promotion, after she had everything sorted and under control—all bases covered, then she'd handle the man-in-her-life challenge.

Tahlia pulled up at the guard's station, rubbing the muscles knotted in her neck. 'Hey, George.' Tahlia slapped her hand on the counter, shooting him a smile. 'Thanks so much again for last night.'

'No problems.' The greying guard shifted his formidable weight in his seat. 'Any time for you. They must give you that promotion soon, eh?'

Tahlia nodded, the buzz of her imminent success in climbing another rung coursing through her. 'Absolutely. It's so close, George, I can smell it.'

George smiled up at her, his cheeks creasing in full waves of doughnut crescents. 'Better not to be late, then.'

'Have a great day.' She swung around, glancing at her watch, striding forward. George was right. If Raquel was looking for a reason not to promote her there was no way in the world she'd give her the satisfaction.

The job was so hers.

She connected with a wall of warm flesh and the scent of soapy clean male engulfed her.

Tahlia looked down, finding her footing and the guy's shiny black, very expensive-looking shoes. His suit trousers were black, stretching up long legs that tapered to a nice flat waist.

His soft blue shirt was covered by a black suit jacket that was tailored to perfection, emphasising just how wide the guy's shoulders were.

His tie was the colour of sapphires…she lifted her gaze…as were his eyes, that met hers with a casual assurance that touched his lips, firm and sensual and full of promises.

Tahlia's breath caught in her lungs.

She shook herself. She was going to stay focused and on track, no matter how short-back-and-sides, clean-shaven, suit-obsessed, white-collar-cute he looked.

'Hello,' he offered, his voice rich and deep, flowing over her like liquid Swiss chocolate. The world tipped.

The man caught her arm, holding her steady, a flash of concern in his gaze. 'Are you okay?'

His hand was strong, hot and muddling. Blood rushed to Tahlia's face, filling her head with a blurring that she couldn't afford right now.

She forced her knees to straighten, strengthen, to not fall for a ridiculous weakness that only happened in a twelve-year-old girl's dreams.

'Yes. Of course. I'm fine,' she managed, lifting her chin and shooting him a smile of cool assurance. 'Loose heel, that's all.'

She cast a glance downward to her black heels, willing that one would fall off gracefully and save her from this embarrassment.

His gaze followed, coursing over her suit jacket, down her simple white blouse, over her short black skirt that stopped a good six inches above her knees, down her bare legs to her feet.

His eyes glinted and she had the sudden urge to cross her arms. She felt naked, as though he'd just seen far more of her than he should have. And liked what he saw.

Butterflies swarmed in her belly.

Tahlia jerked her hand up to her face, pushed back her blonde-streaked long fringe and pointed to the lifts. 'Must go. Love to…' Die on the spot. 'But can't be late for work.'

The cute-suit raised an eyebrow, his blue eyes flashing. 'That's it?'

She froze. What? Did he mean to suggest that he was well aware of her disgusting weak-kneed reaction and was expecting her to fall into his arms again? What arrogance!

'*It?*' she enunciated clearly, crossing her arms. What else could he want? 'As opposed to, *what?*'

'An apology.'

'Oh.' The sound escaped her throat. Of course he did. Obviously. Manners. Why hadn't she thought of that instead of jumping to erogenous conclusions? 'Sorry for—'

His mouth quirked, fighting what looked to be a smile.

She stiffened, her blood heating anew. 'Sorry

for…running into someone who was obviously not looking where *he* was going.'

'Either,' he added, his voice an octave deeper.

'Either,' she echoed as casually as she could, hating to concede a point, and more than infuriated at her body's total lack of sense. 'Fine, but since you agree that you weren't looking where you were going *either*, you could apologise…'

His eyes sparkled. 'You're absolutely right, but I was brought up to believe in "ladies first".'

'I think that relates to entries, exits and queues, not to apologies.' She glared up at him. 'And you have to admit that men need all the practice they can get.'

The man put down his case. 'Apologising?'

She nodded. 'It's really something they don't do enough of.'

'Bad day?' He slipped his hands into his pockets. 'Has your husband upset you?'

She shook her head, a smile jumping to her mouth. 'I'm not married.' Gawd, no. She wasn't going anywhere near *that* challenge for a long time.

'Your boyfriend, then?'

'No—' Tahlia took a step back, her stomach fluttering as though there were a thousand butterflies in it. Was he interested, in *her*? 'Look, I have to go or I'll be late and you don't know my boss—'

He didn't know *her* either.

'She doesn't let you forget any transgression, no matter how insignificant, and it's not like she'll be sympathetic to my bumped-into-a-cute-guy-in-the-lobby excuse, even though she is seriously in need of a good—'

'You think I'm cute?'

She touched her lips. Oh, damn. That couldn't have been her. She never babbled, let alone incoherently. She never put her feet anywhere except where she wanted to go.

She pointed to the lifts, opening her mouth, but no words would come out. What in blazes was going on with her?

'See you around then?' he offered, his warm mouth fighting a smile that promised to be as amazing as the rest of him.

She nodded, swung around and forced herself to get as much distance between them as possible, counting her steps, measuring her speed to look as little like the hasty escape it was as possible.

What was that?

Tahlia shook her head. She wasn't going to even think about it. So, the guy was cute and lust was a natural response. She didn't have to concern herself about a bit of lust and there were so many reasons to lust for that guy.

Deep sexy voice, gorgeous body, tall, commanding and handsome as hell, but she wasn't about to listen to inappropriate primal urges.

She needed a list of criteria for the most appropriate partner, a conservative, safe plan to dating, a timetable that would fit in with her commitments and work demands. This was not the time to get distracted or fall for anyone willy-nilly.

She stepped into the lift, taking a deep slow breath. What was she even thinking? One thing she was sure of. She was never going to *fall* for anyone, especially someone like that.

She was not going to make the same mistakes as her mother. No way in hell.

Case Darrington punched the lift button, unable to stop the smile that had crept on to his lips at meeting the most beautiful woman he'd ever laid eyes on.

It wasn't just her looks. It was everything about her.

The way she'd pulled her short chestnut-brown hair up and back into a wild and spiky knot intrigued him, suggesting a conservative layer covering something untamed underneath.

The large chunk of hair that she left loose could be called a fringe, hanging down and cupping her cheek like his hands itched to.

Her skin had beckoned to him, creamy smooth. Her lips, full and plump like peaches just begging to be tasted. Her eyes, deep dark green, pinning him to the spot.

So much to explore…who was she?

He should have asked her name, should have skipped getting exact directions from the guard and just followed her. He should have kept her talking instead of letting her have her escape without even getting her name, her floor, a glass shoe.

Case put his attaché case by his feet and tried to stop smiling. Hell. She'd floored him, with her eyes, her lips, her words…

Case couldn't say when he'd last been so flattered so simply. Had watched such a beautiful display of…innocent reaction.

He stiffened. What was he thinking? He wasn't about to get carried away with any unusual aches in the heart that he'd thought had died on him.

He'd grown wiser the hard way.

The doors opened on the lift and he snatched up his attaché case and stepped in. He wasn't here for anything but work.

He gripped his case tighter, the woman's face leaping into his mind, her green eyes sizzling and her full lips taunting him.

Dammit. Why couldn't life be as straightforward as figures on a balance sheet?

A woman with deep red hair swept into the small space. 'Hello, handsome,' she lilted.

Case turned to find fluttering lashes on dark eyes that were drinking him up.

He stepped back. That tone…that look…sent memories flashing through the gashes in his heart.

'Are you visiting or are you planning to stay around and make all my dreams come true?' she asked softly, her smile widening, showing teeth.

'I work here,' he said bluntly, staring at the lift doors, willing the thing to get to his floor faster. He'd have to look into that. The lift was too slow. Employees needed to get to their floors much faster, especially when accompanied by predatory females.

She waved a hand laden with gold jewellery, the bracelets tinkling. 'I think I'd remember you unless you have that whole Clark Kent-Superman thing going,' she purred softly, sidling closer to him. 'So are you Clark, or are you my Superman? I do love games.'

'I'm new.' And he hated games. He'd seen enough

games to last him a lifetime. Hell, his ex had been a master at them, playing him in ways he'd never believed possible.

She ran a hand along his jacket sleeve, leaning closer, affording him a generous view of her low-cut blouse and the assets heaving there. 'I could show you around.'

'I don't think so, Miss—?' He stared at the panel—the floor he wanted was the only one lit. Please let it be a mistake, let her not be working with him… The last thing he needed was a constant reminder of his biggest failure in life to date.

She giggled softly as though she hadn't heard his denial. 'Call me Chrystal. And you are?'

The lift chimed.

'Darrington,' Case blurted, striding forward.

The doors opened just in time and he kept moving. He couldn't wait to get as much distance as possible between himself and that man-eater.

He only wished he could escape the memories of his failed marriage as easily.

CHAPTER TWO

The Beatles say all you need is love...
I say give me bug spray.

TAHLIA slapped her handbag on to her desk and swept up the files in one deft move, taking a deep breath and lifting her chin, the echo of her babbling bombarding her senses. What was that?

She was never like that. How embarrassing. She cast her eyes to the ceiling. Please let her not be so stupid again.

She glanced around her office, one wall full of filing cabinets, one with potted plants and paintings, one covered in current jobs and timelines and one made of glass with a great view of the lifts.

She shook her head and swept out of the door, striding down the aisle between the cubicles, replaying that débâcle over again in her mind. The floor could have done her one little favour and swallowed her up before she'd made such a complete and utter fool of herself. Cripes. How old *was* she?

She was far too old to be acting like a schoolgirl, that was for sure. Thank goodness that Emma and Keely hadn't seen that deplorable display. She had a reputation to uphold. Cool, calm and always in control Tahlia Moran, soon to be Marketing Executive.

She swung into the last cubicle. 'Morning, Susan,'

she offered, handing the young woman who was just sitting down a file. 'Could you put some ideas together for this client? They want to change their look to reflect the new season.'

'Sure.'

Tahlia nodded, striding down the row, doling out the updates for existing clients wanting changes to their websites and the assignments for potential clients.

She juggled the files in her arms. There were things a would-be executive did not do, and one was running off at the mouth in emotionally charged situations. Not that she was admitting there was anything but an over-active imagination and a neglected personal life at the root of that particular encounter downstairs.

Two years since her last real date wasn't *that* long, not when she was ensuring a successful career for her future.

She clutched the files remaining. It didn't matter anyway. Downstairs had been nothing but an anomaly. She wasn't going to have to deal with *that* guy, or that abhorrent lack of control again.

'Hey, you,' Tahlia offered Emma, stepping into her friend's cubicle and dropping the files on her desk. '*Flirt* magazine's next issue—they want their update to match the theme and want another competition page designed and put on the site.'

Emma took the file. 'Sure thing.' The glow of love was bright in her eyes. 'Did you hear? It's time. Your day.'

Tahlia shook herself. 'Em?'

'Haven't you logged on yet?' Emma shot her a quiz-zical look. 'Raquel just sent out a mass email to everyone for a meeting in the conference room at half past. Sounds like it could be *it*.'

Tahlia shook her head, kicking herself for not going through her normal routine—checking her voicemail, SMS and inboxes, both cyber and deskbound.

'And?'

'And the whispers suggest it's about the Marketing Exec position.'

Tahlia's belly fluttered. 'She's made a decision? Finally?'

'Yep, it sounds like the Rottweiler has come through. So you'd better get spruced up.' Emma tossed her blonde bob, her smile widening. 'Now you don't have any excuses not to get out there.'

'Out there,' Tahlia echoed, the words ricocheting down her spine, making her skin gooseflesh and the image of that cute-suit bounce around her brain.

'Out there dating. Sheesh, Tahlia, anyone would think from the look on your face that you're not keen to find Mr Right.' Emma clapped her hands. 'I've asked Harry and he has a couple of single mates and Keely says Lachlan is thinking about the possibilities for you too. It would be just perfect if you had someone special to come to my wedding with.'

Tahlia opened her mouth and closed it. What could she say? She had wonderful, interfering, matchmaking-maniac friends who were dying for her to find happiness like they had.

'May I?' she asked slowly, gesturing to the keyboard. Could the promotion really be hers today? Could she dare to believe it finally had come?

Emma rolled her chair away from her desk. 'You have to see it to believe it, right?'

Tahlia stepped forward, clutching the mouse and logging on, clicking her way to her inbox. 'The wording, the tone, the undertones could all mean so much…'

'You're still worried about the rumours that the company isn't going so well?'

Tahlia glanced at her friend. 'You know as well as I do that the whispers suggest jobs are to be axed and no one can deny the fears spreading are of a major shake-up or shake-down.'

'And the latest gossip is that the owners have drawn too much of the cash flow out of the company to fund their overseas romps and WWW Designs is going down, down, down,' Emma said dramatically.

'That's over-exaggeration if ever I heard it.'

Emma nodded, her eyes wide. 'I know.'

TO: *TahliaM@WWWDesigns.com*
CC: *allstaff@WWWDesigns.com*
FROM: *RaquelW@WWWDesigns.com*
SUBJECT: Meeting
All staff,
Be advised that the meeting at 9am in the conference room is mandatory for all staff to be advised of the latest developments.
Don't be late.
Raquel Wilson
General Manager

Tahlia sighed. 'It doesn't say anything regarding my promotion.'

'What else could it be?'

'The possibilities are endless, Em. It could be a new client coming on board, it could be about the rumours, it could be anything.'

'But it could be your promotion. The Rottie always holds an all-staff meeting for changes in personnel.'

Tahlia straightened Em's files on her desk. Was there a reason to get her hopes up? Was it about the position for Marketing Executive?

If it was, there was no one else suitable for the job *so* it had to be her. A bubble of excitement rose up in her chest.

Emma stood up, slapping her on the shoulder. 'Come on. It is *so* about your promotion. It has to be.' She grinned. 'And now you have no excuse to get serious about that part of your life you've put on hold while you got your career *all solid and stable*.'

A chill raced down Tahlia's back.

She smoothed down her suit jacket, shaking off the feeling. It would be fine. 'Yes, not a problem,' she stated casually to her friend. A relationship didn't have to mean disaster, as long as it didn't involve rash decisions, irrational emotions or incredibly embarrassing interactions with too-cute guys.

'You don't sound so sure.'

Tahlia raised her eyebrows, forcing a smile to her mouth. 'I'll handle it like I've handled everything—with criteria, a plan of action and safeguards.'

You could never have too many safeguards, as her mother had shown her. Her mother hadn't considered any were necessary, that love was enough...and it was *so* not enough.

'O-kay,' Em offered, shooting her an odd look, moving out of her cubicle. She glanced at her watch. 'So are you ready for the meeting?'

'Absolutely.' She *was* ready for her dream to come true and Em was right—what else could it possibly be about?

Nothing she couldn't handle.

Tahlia pushed open one of the conference room doors and slipped inside with Emma behind her, weaving through the throng of people, keeping to the wall side of the large room.

She concentrated on the acceptance speech that she'd been practising for months and not on the expanse of glass and views of Melbourne on the far side.

She looked behind her but couldn't see Emma.

Her stomach churned with butterflies. This was going to be the highlight of her year and she damned well deserved it. Why Raquel had waited until now was beyond her.

This was it.

She smiled and her mind filled with all the congratulations that everyone would offer, the sweet proof that Raquel acknowledged her skills and her potential, the incredible thrill of telling her mother she'd finally made it another rung up the ladder.

Raquel cleared her throat, dropping a large folder on the table.

The room fell silent.

'Okay. Thanks for coming, staff,' she said in her trademark nasal bellow. 'Of course you all know that the position of Marketing Executive has been open for some time and is long overdue being filled. I am pleased to announce that a decision has been reached—'

Tahlia held her breath, searching the crowd for her best friends, finding friendly faces with smiles as wide as her own must be.

Emma had been right. This was it—her dream realised, her goal achieved, vindication for endless overtime and a landmark achievement that would ensure that she'd never have to do it hard like her mother.

So what if Emma was getting married and moving to New York to a new job with the love of her life and Keely was taking maternity leave—*she* would have her promotion.

She swung her attention back towards Raquel.

Sapphire-blue eyes caught hers.

Her heart missed a beat.

It was him.

The cute-suit looked taller, dwarfing the staff around him at the head of the table near Raquel the Rottie, standing out all the more in that tailored black suit, the strong lines of his face resembling more a Greek god than…was he an employee of WWW Designs?

What was he doing here? She hadn't heard of anyone being taken on lately, especially a tall, dark and devastating thirty-something.

'Let me introduce to you our new Marketing Executive…' Raquel paused for effect, shooting Tahlia a tight smile, sweeping her hand past Tahlia to the cute-suit. 'Case T Darrington.'

Tahlia's heart slammed against her chest and sank

to the pit of her belly where all the butterflies dropped dead, adding to the weight.

Her vision blurred, her throat closing over. It couldn't be. No. It wasn't possible. There had to be a mistake.

Not him.

Not anybody.

It should have been her!

Raquel put up open arms, her smile wide, avoiding meeting Tahlia's gaze. 'Welcome to the great team here at WWW Designs.'

Tahlia dragged in a slow ragged breath, fighting the sting behind her eyes. How…?

The man behind Raquel sidled out into the open, putting his hands up and rotating slowly like a prize-fighter who'd just knocked out the competition. And he had. Effortlessly.

Her.

CHAPTER THREE

All men are created equal.
But what about women? And are we talking sexism here or feminism-gone-crazy? Has Raquel hired this cute-suit because there are just too many women in the company? Or just because she doesn't want me?

CASE moved to the head of the table, smiling at the new faces around him, taking in the pause after Raquel's announcement, the hesitant applause, the expressions being cast from face to face.

It was to be expected. They had probably figured the position would be filled in-house by someone they already knew who wouldn't question or threaten their way of doing things. And he'd just thrown them out of that comfort zone by being thrown into the mix.

A new face. A loose cannon. Someone who they weren't sure of. *If only they knew.*

'Thank you, Raquel,' he offered the woman who the vision-from-the-lobby had mentioned earlier.

And then there she was, in the audience. He tore his gaze from her, the fact that she worked for him sending warning signals.

'Hello, everyone,' he said smoothly, moving up beside Raquel. 'I'm thrilled to be here and look forward to working with you all. I hope in the coming days to meet you all personally.'

Case glanced towards the beauty again; her face was a mask of professional curiosity. He straightened his tie. Yes. It was time to get serious. He wasn't here to get distracted by a pretty face. He was here to sort out one-hell-of-a-mess.

The challenge was what he needed, had needed since his marriage breakdown, and he'd excelled at finding them. He'd gone out of his way to be involved in the most complicated business deals, play the most exacting sports and pursue the most beleaguered companies.

Since his marriage, women were the one area where he went for simple. Easy, light liaisons with pretty socialites thrilled to be on his arm.

Case scanned the room. WWW Designs was in a perfect mess too. Enough to keep him in busy excuses for not having time for a personal life. And enough to redeem himself for the tragedy his marriage became.

Hell, the look on his parents' faces when he had told them it was over had been the worst part of the whole affair. They prided themselves on their thirty-five years of respectable and spotless marriage, had wished him the same fortunate alliance—the only blemish now was their only child's marital failure.

It was years ago now, but he still hated the feeling of disappointing them.

Case shook his hands out from the balls they'd curled into. He fixed a soft smile to his face and took a breath. 'I've heard great things about the team here at WWW Designs and I'd like to say that I'm very keen on hearing *your* ideas on making improvements, not only in your department, but to make this company even greater.'

Raquel moved forward. 'Thank you, Mr Darrington. I'm sure everyone can't wait to share their thoughts with you,' she barked, shooting a hard look around the room. 'And I'm sure you're eager to get started.'

'That I am,' he said, running his eyes over the crowded room, resting on a pair of very fine green eyes.

'Wonderful. Great. Then let's get on to housekeeping. Tahlia, where are we at on hooking the contracts for the private schools' websites? Mr Darrington, this is Tahlia Moran, Director of Sales.'

Tahlia Moran, aka The Beauty, stepped forward, her shoulders thrown back, her chin high, a chilling blankness in her green eyes that pierced his own for a moment.

Case tossed her name around in his head. It suited her…sweet like her voice and her reaction to him, and strong like the way she held herself and that look.

What was with that look?

She swung her focus to Raquel Wilson. 'We've submitted our ideas to the various schools that were looking and are awaiting their respective decisions,' she said in a cold, lifeless monotone.

His gut tightened.

The woman he'd bumped into downstairs had glowed with such passion that he could imagine clients swarming towards her like bees to spring blossoms.

What was going on in the office to cause such a turn-around in her? Case scanned the room. How many others here were having their enthusiasm sucked out of them? And by what?

He had to find out.

The company's future success could hinge on him sorting it out—and he knew just where to start. With a tall, dazzling mystery that begged to be explored.

He just wasn't sure whether he should.

Tahlia stared at her computer screen, willing the words to clear so she could read her mail and get on with the job she still had.

TO: *TahliaM@WWWDesigns.com*
CC: *KeelyR@WWWDesigns.com*
FROM: *EmmaR@WWWDesigns.com*
SUBJECT: A crazy crazy world

Missed you at the end of the meeting. I expect you needed some space. Gawd, Tahlia. I'm so sorry.

There must be some reason the Rottie chose that creep over you. Maybe there's something going on with them—he is rather cute for a creep.

I think the world has gone crazy. First your promotion goes to some total stranger and then Chrystal. I just had the weirdest talk with her about men. No. Not about size. Or quality. Or quantity. She was asking my advice on how to land Mr Right! Freaky, huh? I guess our office nymph has decided, finally, that she wants more than just sex from men.

What do you think Darrington's T stands for?
Tyrant?

Em

And if you need to talk, or scream or yell or cry,
I'm here for you, sweetie.

Tahlia threw herself back in her chair, staring at the
ceiling. Yes, the guy was a creep, sauntering into the
building, flaunting his good looks, great suit and that
sexy mouth and sharing that oh-so-deep voice.

Acting as if he was just anybody when innocent
hard-working employees bumped into him was wrong,
and totally inappropriate behaviour in the circumstances.

The nerve of the guy to meet her gaze in the meeting, all warm and soft, as though he was naïve and
innocent and ignorant to the fact that it was her promotion he'd stolen.

He didn't need the job. With a suit that expensive it
was surprising he was working at all. *He* probably had
a silver spoon stuck well and truly up his—

She slammed a fist on her desk. He probably wasn't
even qualified, had probably figured there was nothing
wrong with using his wealth and connections to jump
over hard-working employees on his ruthless climb to
the top.

She'd hardly heard his acceptance, but had seen him
smiling at her, as though his stealing her job wasn't
enough, that he had to rub salt deep into the wounds
of her dashed hopes and dreams.

Bastard. After she had been so stupid and babbling
and stupid downstairs.

Gawd. He was her boss now. He was probably going to sack her…especially after what she had said about Raquel…unless he had already told Raquel. Then that was it, she was dead—the Rottie would eat her alive!

How could she have messed this up so badly?

How could she have failed?

Everything had been going so well. She'd had everything under control… How could she not have twigged that the Rottie was interviewing other candidates for the promotion she desperately wanted?

Tahlia cringed. How could she have let her mouth run away with her with the one person who should have seen her as absolutely together?

At least she'd reported the update without revealing a shred of the turmoil that raged within her. She was well practised at keeping it all deep inside.

Dammit. Her mother hadn't let anything get in her way to the top—not her grief, the rumours, motherhood, her limited education, nothing.

She straightened the photo on her desk of her mother in her favourite power suit with her arms crossed and chin up.

It had taken her mother over a year to save up enough for that suit. Tahlia had watched her come home from the supermarket every day, take off her uniform, make dinner and then iron, and study and iron, and go to night school and iron.

Her mother had said her power suit was forged by iron, and was therefore even more charged to give her the boost in business she needed.

Her mother had taught her about goals and strength

and determination and, dammit, she wasn't going to just give in.

She was a professional, like her mother, and she was going to hold her head high and deal with what life threw at her. Hell, she was used to it. Life had thrown a few big ones their way and they'd not only survived, they'd got stronger.

Even the rumours about Tahlia's dad hadn't stopped her mother—if anything they had driven her. Her mother's passion had inspired Tahlia…and Tahlia was not a quitter like her father. She was a winner, a survivor, and totally in control of her own life…and its surprises.

She'd survive this like she had survived everything else in her life to date—she just didn't know how to tell her mother…

Tahlia picked up a pen and stabbed the notepad in front of her. Damn that man. Damn Raquel. Damn the world.

How could this happen…right when she was going to prove that she'd be okay, that she was somebody too, that she'd made it?

Life wasn't fair.

Who was that man?

Sammy's, their local coffee shop, was busy in the afternoons but perfect for the quick after-work drink Tahlia and the girls had before they headed home.

Sammy's was mandatory to catch up on the weekend goss if they hadn't got the chance at work. Most days they'd go the entire day and not get to talk, depending on their work commitments, like the rest of today.

Although Tahlia had to admit she hadn't been so much working as hiding in her office, smothering her thoughts with work rather than trying to make sense of this disastrous turn of events.

She pushed open the coffee shop door, glancing at her watch. She was late. Maybe late enough for the girls to be totally focused on the wedding or the baby shower and to have forgotten entirely about her lack of promotion.

She didn't want to talk about it. She wanted to forget it had happened, try to recapture that naïve innocence and faith she'd had this morning that it was imminent, not an 'if' but a 'when' and she was the success she wanted to be.

Tahlia weaved through the tables. She definitely didn't want to talk about it until she knew what in heavens she was going to do about it.

Keely and Emma were leaning over their usual table, looking up at the same time, as though they'd picked her up on some radar.

'I'm so sorry, honey,' Emma said, gathering up the photos of wedding cakes and a couple of dozen letters that were probably more of the RSVPs she'd been checking off her guest list for the last week. 'About the promotion.'

Tahlia slid into the seat at the booth, gesturing for Andy, their usual waiter. 'It's nothing. A slight hiccup. I'll be fine.' She wished she could feel as fine as she hoped she sounded.

'Darrington is one hell of a hiccup.'

Tahlia shook her head, swallowing hard. 'So your baby shower is next week—' And then she'd be abandoning work for putting her feet up and focusing on her future, her baby, her husband and her new house.

'And you're avoiding the subject. What are you going to do about the new suit in the office?' Keely asked, tipping her head.

'Nothing,' Tahlia said as casually as she could, shrugging. 'I'm going to ignore him.'

Emma tapped her pile of stuff into symmetry. 'That may be a bit difficult seeing as he's your boss.'

'And he's cute as,' Keely added.

'I'm a professional.' And there was no way she wanted to see the guy again after their mortifying first meeting, let alone the fact he'd destroyed her dream.

Keely leant forward in her seat, her hand resting on her bulge. 'So you're telling us that you haven't noticed how nice-looking he is?'

She shook her head vigorously. 'No.' She wished she'd known who the guy was from the start so she hadn't allowed her body to buzz around in flights of fancy. 'I don't find that sort of clean-cut chiselled features, tailored-suit sort of guy attractive at all.' *Now*.

Today was just another good reason to avoid men altogether—they were trouble. They took what you wanted and ruined your life.

Emma drained her cup. 'So what now?'

'I get on with my job,' Tahlia said coolly, raising her eyebrows and giving a soft shrug. What else could she do?

'If we still have one,' Keely offered, flicking cookie crumbs from the table in front of her. 'Rumour has it that the owners are selling up WWW.'

'That one has been going around for ages,' Tahlia retorted, fighting the ache in her belly. It couldn't happen, not to her workplace, *her* future…

Keely got up, picking up her coat. 'I've got to go…home to Lachlan—gosh, I still can't believe my luck.'

'You deserve it,' Tahlia offered, grabbing her friend's hand and giving it a quick squeeze. 'And more.'

Emma shoved her wedding stuff into her large bag. 'You know you could start looking around for another job?'

Tahlia shook her head. 'I've got too much invested here.' And she'd rather walk on hot coals than admit failure, especially to her mum. She was going to get that promotion even if she had to wait another year for it.

'But don't feel bad that you're running off to the Big Apple.' Tahlia slapped the back of her hand to her forehead dramatically. 'Leaving me all on my own to battle the Darrington disaster.'

Emma laughed. 'You'll do just fine.'

Tahlia nodded, forcing a smile to her face. 'Of course. Always.' She was always fine. She had been fine when her father had died, fine when her mother had gone to work, fine when she'd come home to an empty house, fine when her mother hadn't made it to

her graduation, her birthdays or their lunch-dates, and
she was fine now.

She could handle Darrington all on her own. She'd
find out who the man was and what he'd done so that
she could explain how he could get her job promotion—to herself and to her mother.

Maybe he just had better luck than her. She bit her
bottom lip. Maybe she should get a few charms to be
on the safe side, to cover all bases, to ensure her
success.

She'd do anything to get where she wanted to go.
She was a professional.

CHAPTER FOUR

Everything in life has a price.
And I never know what it is until it's too late.

CASE sat in the large leather chair and surveyed his new office again. He couldn't quite believe he was here.

He'd spent all yesterday calling in employees, talking to them, encouraging them to tell him just how much they did in the company and how much more they could do, given the right incentives.

Work was going well.

This was going to be good for him. It reminded him of where he'd been six years ago, took him back to simpler times, when he still believed in so many things, including love and marriage.

Framed prints hung on the walls, large ferns sat in the corners looking as if they were in need of a water or a wax—he never could tell if indoor plants were fake or not—the sofa in the corner was cream with tan cushions that matched the rug under the glass and chrome coffee table.

The place could do with a makeover, as one of the employees had suggested, to improve morale. He'd have to look into it. And Miss Tahlia Moran.

Case snatched a pen from the desk, slapping it into his palm. No. There was no mystery to unravel.

Nothing to explore except how to get this office dynamic working to its highest potential.

The only responsibility he had was to the company. So what if she'd vanished during the meeting yesterday, somewhere after her report and the general housekeeping.

He stabbed the pen into the file on his desk. He wished she'd left his thoughts as easily. He couldn't stop wondering about her and that lack of light in her eyes.

He'd half thought of calling her into his office yesterday but had caught himself. There was no rush here—he could take his time to investigate the office politics, the hierarchies and issues at WWW. Besides, he would run into her eventually. They were on the same floor.

But he hadn't yesterday.

Was she avoiding him? He rubbed his jaw. She could easily be. Women were strange creatures. She could be put out that he hadn't mentioned his position to her when he'd bumped into her. But dammit, he hadn't wanted anything to interfere with her first impressions of him. It was so rare for him to have people see him as himself.

For once in his life he just wanted to be Joe Anybody.

Much good it had done him. He was her boss now, and the cool professional look she had cast him across the boardroom yesterday had said it all.

'Mr Darrington,' Miss Moran offered, tapping on his door. 'You wanted to see me?'

She stood tall with high black heels, black trousers

that held her curves and a white shirt with the top buttons undone, giving the hint of a lace undershirt.

His blood heated.

Her hair was in the same wild knot as yesterday, her lips were pursed, her green eyes cool and assessing, a finely arched eyebrow quirking as though she was not impressed to be here.

'Yes.' Case cracked his knuckles. He'd spent the last twenty-four hours trying to work out *why* it mattered so much what she thought of him...

He moved around his desk, extending his hand, offering it to her. 'Case.'

She nodded.

'And you are Tahlia Moran, Director of Sales,' he suggested lightly.

She raised her eyes to meet his. 'Guilty,' she said, striding forward and taking his hand.

Heat sizzled up his arm. 'Nice shake, Miss Moran.'

She pulled her hand from his smoothly. 'Ditto, Mr Darrington.'

'Call me Case.'

Tahlia stepped back. 'I have to say...before... downstairs...you caught me off-guard. I'm usually quite...sane.'

'O-kay,' he murmured, watching the rise of colour in her cheeks. Was she embarrassed?

His body buzzed at the thought. *Did* she like him? Had she felt the heat between their palms too? Had she felt that buzz yesterday when they'd collided?

Was that why she was so upset that he was her boss—because she felt the electricity between them but maybe had her own rules for not getting involved with workmates?

Hell, he had the same ideals. But if there could be one person he'd compromise his rules for it would be her, and that incredibly sweet innocence that she'd just bubbled with yesterday morning.

Now he'd never know...anything she said would be sugar-coated for 'the boss'.

Case straightened his tie. He was giving himself a headache. There was only one way to find out what was going on with Tahlia Moran and put his mind at rest...

He just hoped he liked the answers.

Tahlia glared at the man standing behind *her* desk in *her* office with *her* title as casually and comfortably as though he owned the place. 'If we could make this quick, Mr Darrington, I have work to do.'

He lifted an eyebrow. 'Would you like a coffee?' he asked, reducing the distance between them. 'I'm just on my way to the kitchenette.'

'Fine,' she bit out, stepping well back for the man to pass by. She didn't want to be anywhere near the guy, let alone touch him again.

She swiped her hand against her thigh, trying to dispel the tingling in her palm.

He stopped beside her. 'Ladies first,' he said smoothly, gesturing the way for her.

'Fine.' She sauntered down the hall, her breathing short and shallow, her hands clenched tightly at her sides. The promotion-stealer *had* to remind her of yesterday morning's embarrassment!

Wasn't it enough that he'd started throwing his weight around? Meeting everyone under him and convincing them he was interested in their ideas.

Jerk.

So, it was a great idea, not only to meet his staff but to get friendly and supportive…especially since he was a stranger coming in, but if he was thinking it was going to be easy to get on her good side he had another think coming.

Tahlia pushed open the door on the kitchenette and stalked across the room to get as much distance between them as she could. 'So what can I do for you, Mr Darrington?'

'Call me Case,' he said again smoothly, striding to the coffee pot and picking it up with one hand, plucking a mug from the rack with the other. 'How would you like it?'

She crossed her arms over her chest, resisting a reaction to his casual friendliness, his supposed humility in the face of his superior position, the ease with which he brandished the coffee pot as though it was natural to him to make his own.

Tahlia stiffened. 'How would I like it?' Pretending to be just another workmate was *not* going to get him anywhere with her. 'I think honestly and straight down the line,' she said evenly. 'No sugar-coating or fluffy padding would be nice.'

'I meant your coffee, but okay…' He smiled, his blue eyes gleaming at her.

Tahlia swallowed down the flutter in her belly. Snap out of it. So he was in a kick-arse deep blue suit that hugged his body like silk to pillows. So his eyes smiled as sexily as his mouth. She was *not* going to make any mistakes today. 'Black, no sugar.'

Darrington nodded. 'I need to know all about my staff. My team. I'm reliant on them to make or break this company,' he said, splashing the coffee into her mug and sliding it down the bench to her.

She halted its progress, cupping the mug in her hand. 'It sounds like you're aiming at Raquel's job next,' she said slowly. He couldn't take that off her too... 'A little ambitious for the first week, aren't you?'

He put the coffee pot back, poured some milk in his mug and added three spoons of sugar. 'I like to aim high. I like to push my staff to their potential and I like to succeed.'

She nodded tightly. WWW Designs sure needed that sort of attitude, that optimism and drive...but from her, not some interloper!

Case Darrington sipped his coffee. 'So what do you have to offer, Miss Moran?'

She paused, her nerves rippling their response down her spine and settling deep in her belly. 'My track record speaks for itself, Mr Darrington,' she bit out. She'd be damned if she was going to spell out her worth to a man who had undermined it.

He leant against the counter, his attention fixed entirely on her. 'I want to hear it from you.'

Tahlia took a deep breath. 'Well, that's all well and fine but I'm a busy woman. I really don't have time to list my skills, my achievements and my worth to this company to somebody who can't be bothered reading my file.'

His mouth fought a smile. 'You're not scared of me?'

She took a gulp of the coffee and looked pointedly at her watch. 'No.'

'Not even wary?'

'No.'

He crossed his arms over his wide chest. 'Aren't you worried I'll fire you for your lack of respect for authority?'

Tahlia shrugged. 'If you can't see my worth from reading my file, by what I do around here, then I'm better off somewhere else.'

He nodded slowly, his mouth fighting a smile. 'You are absolutely right.'

She met his sapphire-blue eyes warily. 'I am?' What was he up to? It had to be something...

'Yes.' He picked up his mug and walked to the door. 'Maybe we can discuss any ideas you have...over lunch some time?'

'Ye-es,' she said slowly. She had a lot of ideas to improve the place that Raquel hadn't seemed to want to hear despite numerous discussions, letters, memos and slip-anonymous-suggestions-on-to-her-desk attempts.

It would be nice to have someone who was actually open to improvement rather than just wanting to keep doing things the way they had always been done because it was *her* way.

Tahlia surveyed the man in front of her. Did the Rottie have any idea what this new guy was up to? She couldn't wait to see her face when Darrington brought her his recommendations to change her system.

She caught herself. Darn it. He wasn't meant to be like this, all competent and businesslike and friendly.

He was meant to be an insensitive jerk who didn't really care about anything but his own career.

He was…nice, and behaving like one hell of a good boss—if she could trust him. Huh. Like that would ever happen. Tahlia Moran was never going to trust a man.

She wasn't about to weaken, not when so much depended on her being strong, sensible and in control.

'So I'm guessing you'll want to meet to discuss new markets, existing clients and what my team's ideas are to advertise our services?'

Case Darrington shook his head. 'Not a priority for me just now,' he offered casually, and left.

Tahlia stared after him. Not a priority? He didn't want to know about it? What on earth was wrong with the guy? Didn't he have any idea what his job was?

She swung to the sink and tipped the rest of her coffee down the drain and rinsed her cup. This was such a stuff-up!

How could he have been put in that position, *her* position, if he wasn't going to do what was needed?

She strode to the door, her blood hot, her body tense.

This wasn't her failure; it was Raquel's. She was the right person for the job…a mistake had been made. She just had to prove it.

So the new guy thought he was God's gift to the office with his smooth deep voice, friendly act and dazzling blue eyes? So he enjoyed toying with her and watching her embarrass herself?

So Case *Thieving* Darrington liked playing games? She could play a few of her own to find out what she needed.

He wouldn't know what hit him.

CHAPTER FIVE

They say it's lonely at the top.
I say it can be lonely anywhere.

CASE glanced at his watch. What time did they take lunch here? He ran a hand through his hair. He had no idea.

He'd tried to play it cool by waiting, taking his time, attempting to talk himself out of taking the woman to lunch over the last two days, but it was impossible. Everyone he talked to had something to say about Tahlia Moran's dedication and commitment to her work...

He'd cracked and sent an invitation to lunch to her this morning.

He had to know more about her than the snippets he'd picked up in conversation around the office.

It wasn't enough.

There was enough information to go either way. Her dedication to her work intrigued him, her confidence teased him and her beauty tortured every inch of him. But he could be wrong...like with Celia, his ex...and Tahlia's dedication could well border on obsession, her confidence narcissistic and her beauty only skin-deep.

Tahlia's reluctance to pander to him or his ego fascinated him. Her forwardness, her bluntness, her total

43

lack of pretence appealed to something in him. What, he didn't know...

He couldn't afford another mistake. For his parents' wavering belief in him as much as his own reluctance to go through anything like Celia ever again.

So what was he doing? Playing with fire...

He stood up and strode to the floor-to-ceiling window and stared out at the Yarra river and Melbourne's city sprawl on the other side.

Hell, he needed a breath of fresh air in his life. He deserved one after what Celia had put him through.

Celia had been amazing in the beginning, sweeping him off his feet with her calm assurance and big smiling eyes into a whirlwind marriage that had torn through his savings, his illusions and his heart.

He could have gone on for years, trying to make it work, pushing her to see a counsellor with him, attempting to recapture the magic of those early days. Her spending hadn't mattered. He had been making enough to fund her passion for designer clothes, shoes and jewellery.

All he had wanted was for her to love him again.

He hadn't known what he'd done wrong.

Hadn't known what to do next.

He'd gone home early that day to beg for her help in saving their marriage, rekindling the magic, sharing in finding the solution that eluded him. What he'd found was Celia sharing herself with some bronzed stud in their bed.

Case closed his eyes, the image scored in his mind. He was a fool. Even then he would have tried again, would have burdened the blame, just to get her to want to save their marriage as much as he had wanted to.

She hadn't. She'd wanted a divorce, half of what was left of his assets and to be rid of him.

Thanks to several savvy lawyers involved in their pre-marital agreement, she'd only got two out of three.

Case ran a hand through his hair, cringing. It was nearly a year since the divorce had finally been settled. Logic suggested it was long enough to get on with life, but the wounds he bore still ached deep in his chest.

The betrayal was going to take longer to get over and he was strong enough to ignore Tahlia's lush peach lips, those dazzling green eyes, her sweet voice and intriguing focus on business.

The knock startled him. Case turned. Tahlia Moran stood at his door in a short black skirt that showed just how long and shapely her legs were, the slight curve of her hips and her narrow waist.

Her hands were on her hips, her lips pursed. 'Ready, Mr Darrington?' she lilted, her voice sweet as apple blossom.

Maybe not. Case swallowed hard, pulling at his tie and straightening it, his blood roaring hot and fiery through him.

He couldn't deny he was attracted. But he didn't need to take any risks. He could keep it light. Keep it simple. Get to know the woman, with no strings and no complications.

He wasn't going to get distracted from WWW Designs, no matter what Tahlia Moran made him feel.

*   *   *

Tahlia stood in Case *The Target* Darrington's doorway, her cheeks heating under the warmth of his gaze and the way his eyes caressed her.

She could feel everything traitorously warming.

'So?' she offered, crossing the files in her hands over her breasts, lingering in the doorway, grinding her teeth, glaring at the man who had stolen the only thing that really mattered.

Her work was her anchor and the darned waters had changed on her—she was no longer tethered to rock, she was drifting and she hated it.

She'd even emailed the girls an SOS in desperation to get them over to her place tonight to help her with this dilemma.

How was she going to get the information she needed out of the guy? It was one problem she could do with help with.

Tahlia bit her bottom lip. She didn't like asking for help...would play it down tonight and smoothly draw their wisdom without sounding needy.

She didn't need anyone.

He cleared his throat. 'So you're here.'

She nodded, looking away from the window to his paintings on the walls. 'Ye-es.' Did he suspect she was going to give the note a close encounter with the shredder and plead ignorance of receiving it rather than accept his invitation?

But she was a professional who was going to use the opportunity of lunch to find out exactly what was on Case's CV that entitled him to her job.

He stood up. 'Ready for lunch?'

'Sure, but *why* are we going to lunch?' she asked

carefully, keeping her eyes on him and not on the view.

'I really need to come up to speed fast. Find out about the office dynamics as quickly as possible to maximise my position here.'

She couldn't help but smile. He sounded just like she would if she was dropped into his situation, although she would never crush the dreams of someone else who'd earned the promotion through damned hard work.

Darrington straightened his suit jacket, the fabric looking even finer and more expensive as he got closer to her. It must have cost a fortune to have it made from a fabric like that, and to hug his wide shoulders, taunting everyone in the vicinity...

Who was this guy?

She had to find out and then do something about him...

'What?' he asked, his voice deep and husky, his gaze on her mouth.

She shook herself, trying to stop the smile.

His blue eyes glittered. 'Your smile is—'

'Hungry. I'm hungry.' She cast a look at her watch. 'I'll meet you at Sammy's, the coffee shop, in half an hour, okay?'

He nodded, his gaze still on her lips.

She tried to smother the smile, tried to think of something else other than sweet revenge for every thwarted nobody who'd been stomped on by a rich somebody.

She didn't want him to guess what she was up to.

She hoped he liked surprises.

CHAPTER SIX

'I deserve the best and I accept the promotion now.'
Because I'm willing to do whatever it takes, because
I'm worth it, because he's an arrogant, wealthy
sexy-as-hell annoying man who doesn't deserve it.

'So.' TAHLIA handed the menu back to the waitress. 'Apart from being partial to fish and chips, what titbits do you have to share about yourself so I can spread them all over the office by the end of the working day?'

Case put down his lemon squash, trying not to smile at the woman's amazing frankness. Was she for real? He wasn't sure what to make of her or the incredible feeling he had deep inside whenever he was near her.

And she'd said yes. She'd agreed to lunch with him, which could be construed as an indication that she may like him. She had to know as well as he did that they could have discussed anything at the office.

And she was asking a lot of questions. He probably shouldn't see her wanting to know about him as anything more than face-value gossip for the office, but he couldn't help feeling it was more. 'For the record it was a fillet of the finest deep sea dory, garden salad and fries.'

She fixed him with her sea-green gaze. 'So you *are* a snob.'

He leant back in his seat, considering her challenge. 'And you're against snobs?'

'Isn't everyone?' she lilted, raising a finely arched eyebrow at him.

'Well, not the snobs, obviously,' he murmured, his gaze on her glistening peach lips, which were as mesmerising as the words coming from them. No one had challenged him on this level before. Because he was too rich to be a snob or too rich to be called one to his face?

She straightened the cutlery in front of her, her long fringe falling over her right eye. 'Right. Snobs stick together.'

'I'd say so.' He clasped his glass tightly, the urge to smooth that lock of hair back from her face excruciatingly tempting.

'You don't sound so sure. Don't you know a snob, maybe intimately?'

'If you're asking me if I'm a snob, then no, I'm not,' he said as casually as he could, the buzz that she was interested enough to want to know filling his head, and other places.

'Well, a snob *would* say that.' She crossed her arms over her full breasts. 'Where were you born, where did you grow up and where did you go to school?'

Case stared at the dazzling woman opposite. Blunt and forward, like he'd never experienced before. And he wanted to give her all the answers she needed, as honestly as he could, as long as she didn't find out why he was really at WWW.

He took a sip of his drink and placed it down gently on the small round table between them. 'Born to John and Marie Darrington in Melbourne. Was raised modestly in Toorak by said parents. Went to school first at Stott's College then did a business degree at Melbourne University.'

He put up his hands. 'All snob-suggested but, despite my parents' success and standing, I was raised just like a regular kid.'

'Really? And a regular kid is raised how?'

He offered her a smile. It was way too early to get into how much worth his peers and parents had put on money, possessions and connections as he had grown up, especially on how to keep the family 'up there' after his father's new money had got them out of what they called middle class mediocrity. 'How about you?'

'About me?'

'Yes.' He leant forward, tipping his head, trying to catch her gaze from behind that lock of hair. 'I'm interested in knowing all my staff's background.' And hers in particular.

She gave a shrug. 'As I've already said, you could read my file.'

'There's a lot not in a file.' He'd already looked, twice. 'I'd like to hear it from you.'

'Not much to tell. Born and raised in Sydney. Moved to Melbourne after university. My first job was here, and here I still am. I've been with WWW Designs for just over four years, working my way up, putting in the long hours, doing that extra bit to make an impression.'

Case nodded. She'd made an impression on him all right. 'I did the same.' He'd been determined to make his career on his own, refusing his father's help, and putting in the hard work. 'Long hours and that extra commitment is the trick.'

Tahlia cringed. Sure, there was a trick all right, in stealing other people's promotions, and she was going to find out exactly what his was and shove it down his throat.

And he'd missed *her* point entirely. Gawd, a woman would have to put up with a lot being interested in this guy. 'Your someone at home must be very patient with your hours,' she bit out.

'Yes, he is.'

'He?' She froze. Did he live with his father or a room-mate? He looked like a confirmed-bachelor-playboy in a penthouse apartment on the North Shore sort of guy, the sort that liked his own space to do all the entertaining he desired.

'Yes. Couldn't do without him. Fetches my paper, shoes, even finds my car keys when I mislay them,' he said, his deep voice washing over her.

She had known it. A butler. He was a total snob then and the title was especially earned if his money and connections had got him *her* job promotion.

Andy arrived with their orders, slipping the plates in front of them, shooting her a wink.

'Thank you,' she said, straightening her plate in front of her, arranging the grilled chicken burger with salad for easy access of her right hand to maximise efficiency and minimize this lunch with the enemy.

'Thank you,' Case offered Andy, rotating his plate, glancing at Tahlia. 'And he likes bones.'

'Bones?' Tahlia echoed. *What?*

Case grinned. 'My dog, Edison. He's a Border Collie… You're in such a hurry to label me, aren't you?'

A dog? Sheesh. She pushed back her fringe, tucking it behind her ear, feeling the annoying heat in her cheeks. 'You can't say you haven't labelled me.'

'That's true,' he said softly, his gaze coursing over her.

Her blood heated at the thought of what the label was… She didn't want to know, or think about it. 'I have goldfish myself. Low maintenance,' she blurted. 'I did think of getting a cat but then she would have eaten Bert and Ernie, the fish, and although they don't fetch sticks, papers or shoes they do listen very patiently when I get home and need to—'

She pressed her tongue against the roof of her mouth in an attempt to still it. Was she babbling?

'Please, don't stop.'

She lifted her burger and took a large bite, filling her mouth with food instead of a plethora of personal stuff that had no business in her mouth, let alone pouring out.

What was wrong with her?

He watched her.

She chewed, swallowed and sighed. Was it her horoscope messing with her again? 'You're a Leo, right?'

'Sagittarian, I'm told. You?'

'Puzzled at how you came to WWW Designs. I didn't see you come in for an interview for the position and I see most people who come to the floor, not because I'm a busybody or anything, just that my view is of the lift—'

Case swallowed his mouthful. 'I noticed.'

'And?'

He shrugged as though it wasn't important. 'I was out-sourced. Head-hunted. Appropriated by Ms Wilson. I think you're right, by the way. She does seem in need of a good—'

'Mr Darrington...' she rushed in '...you must have met Raquel previously, then, for her to get such a good impression of you to go and steal you from another firm—which one, by the way? One of our rivals?'

He smiled at her. 'I met her...at a...party.'

She was getting nowhere. The man wasn't giving much away at all! Tahlia leant close. '*Are* you the enemy?'

'No.' His mobile rang. 'Sorry, but I have to get it.' He pulled the small handset from his belt. 'Yes... Hello, Simon, everything okay...? Oh...right.' He glanced at Tahlia, then swung to one side of his chair, gazing at his shoes. 'It's not exactly a good time... Fine. I'll try... Go ahead with that... No, not yet on that... I'll get back to you regarding that... Okay... Yes... Look, I'll talk to you later.'

He grinned sheepishly at her, putting the mobile phone down. 'Where were we?'

Tahlia took another mouthful of her lunch, forcing the chicken down her tight throat. Whatever that had been about...she didn't like it. 'What was that? Were you picking horses?'

She mentally prayed. Let him be a gambler, let him be an alcoholic gambler, let him be an alcoholic reckless gambler. That would prove to Raquel what a terrible mistake she'd made.

He shook his head. 'No.'

Tahlia stared at him. 'So it would be—?'

He smiled at her, shrugging. 'Companies.'

'So Simon is your broker?' she asked slowly, trying to match it to what she'd heard. It could have been, but something didn't quite fit.

'For someone professing not to be a busybody you ask a lot of questions.'

'Self-preservation.'

'Oh?'

She took a sip of her water. 'I like to know what I'm getting into, in the office, with the new boss,' she stumbled, the words sounding too…suggestive.

'Oh?' he murmured deeply.

She put her drink down, taking a breath. 'And you haven't told me one thing that supports the fact that you're any way qualified for the job,' she said in a rush. 'Or that your personality would complement the working environment or that there's anything about you that *doesn't* scream silver-spoonfed life, apart from your dog.' And that smile, and those eyes and that deep warm voice.

'Lucky you weren't the one hiring, then.'

She glared at the man opposite, but he was focused on his meal, carefully avoiding her gaze.

Tahlia finished her salad, forcing the food down on to a stomach busy doing somersaults at his every sapphire glance. This wasn't the plan.

She wiped her hands on a serviette and arranged the cutlery carefully on her plate. She was getting nowhere. 'Look, I represent the busybodies of the office and I demand some incredibly personal information that I can share with them that will ensure that you're not only human but approachable, sensible and on-the-whole nice.'

She crossed her fingers under the table. If that wasn't an invitation for him to arrogantly sing his praises and convince her once and for all that he was exactly who she hoped he was, then she didn't know what was.

He stared at her.

His gaze dropped to her mouth.

Visions of his firm, sensual lips smothering hers rocked through her, setting alight every nerve that hadn't already realised he was sitting barely a metre from her.

Hmm, a kiss. That would be personal all right, but not something she could share with the office... She shook herself. Or wanted. She didn't want his mouth on hers, at all, ever.

She dropped her gaze to his mouth, which was firm and enticing.

Kissing the boss would prove that he was a playboy, after short skirts and a good time and not focused on the company's best interests...

Was a kiss what he was thinking of or was she being stupid?

He jerked to his feet. 'You don't think I'm human? Approachable? Nice?' he asked, dropping some money on to the table to cover the meal.

She sucked in a long slow breath, rising from her seat. 'Nothing you've said or done suggests any of the latter,' she said in a rush.

'I've answered every question...' he offered, turning and walking to the door.

She nodded. He had, as easily and openly as though

he were just any other guy, but she knew he wasn't…
There was something that didn't add up with Case
Terrorising Darrington.

'I've just had a very pleasant lunch with you…' He
opened the coffee shop door and held it open for her,
watching her with steady blue eyes.

'Ye-es,' she managed, striding through the door,
smoothing down her skirt, counting her heartbeats with
the clack of her heels on the ground.

She couldn't deny that he was *being* friendly and
nice but that didn't mean he was anything but a good
actor.

Tahlia lengthened her stride, pushed open the door
to their building, holding it for Case this time. The air
was tense between them. 'And—?' she had to ask.

He strode alongside her as they crossed the foyer. A
lift was waiting, its doors open.

Case strode in, punched their floor number and
turned to her. 'Now what can I do to show you I'm
only human?'

Tahlia's glance went straight for his mouth.

Case fought every impulse in his body to reduce the
distance between them, take her into his arms and crush
his mouth to hers.

It was insane.

He'd thought he'd got his instincts under control.
After the disaster that his marriage had turned into, he
would have thought he'd have learned.

He took a deep breath. He wasn't going to rush into
this, no matter what this was.

If he hadn't been so young and naïve four years ago

he wouldn't have ended up with a two-year sentence for stupidity with Celia.

He'd been in such a rush to get married and complete his well-rounded success in all areas of his life he hadn't stopped to think.

The fact that she'd been married once already to another blinded-by-love well-off businessman should have given him fair warning of what he was in for.

He pulled his attention from those lips that were taunting him and those sea-green eyes that seemed to be daring him to take the plunge. 'Tahlia, Miss Moran… I…don't have a personal assistant or secretary.'

She blinked. 'She went when the Executive went, sir,' she said smoothly, her sweet voice hardly registering the look of surprise that showed in her eyes.

'Really?' He cleared his throat, pushing down the heat in his body. Talking shop would dull the senses. 'Why was that?'

'Yes. I believe Raquel can explain your predecessor's departure more appropriately than I can,' she said slowly, staring at the lift doors, her sweet perfume circling around him and taunting him.

It would be so easy to lean over and hit that stop button, sweep her into his arms and taste those lips and feel the passion that lay there, simmering just beneath the surface.

'I want to hear what you have to say,' he asked tightly. Any sort of office history may serve as a distraction to the desire coursing through him.

'He and his secretary had a hot and heavy affair.'

Case stared at the ceiling. Cripes. Just what he

needed to hear. 'And that was frowned upon by company policy?' he asked slowly. And maybe he'd find out Tahlia's policy.

She smoothed down the fabric of her short skirt over gently rounded hips. 'Well, yes. The powers that be don't want office harmony going to hell because of spats between exes and all those favouritism issues that become a factor in intimate relationships, not to mention issues of harassment.'

'That makes sense,' he said softly, forcing his feet to stay where they were and not take him any closer to the woman who was calling him like a siren to the rocks. 'But what do *you* think?'

She moistened her lips and jerked her gaze back to the lift door, holding her hands tightly in front of her. 'Me?' she asked tightly. 'In the end, the staff are all adults…mostly,' she rushed on. 'And it's impossible to police—more a guideline, really. You know, don't mix business and pleasure.'

'Right.'

She sucked in a breath. 'And in that particular instance the pair involved were doing more of the pleasure than business, and not just in his office—'

'O-kay,' Case said, adjusting his belt and taking a step back from Tahlia. 'I get the picture.' Vividly. And his mind filled with all the places they would have gone and visions of him visiting such quiet nooks with the incredible woman next to him.

'Basically it's to dissuade secretaries of the young and idealistic variety from thinking that a fling with the boss is going to help the career,' she blurted, twining her fingers together.

Case couldn't help but smile at her rush of words. Was she nervous?

'Well,' he offered, his voice low. 'You can inform the office and any young and idealistic staff that I'm single. But I can assure you that I will not give my assistant any illusions about climbing the ladder through sexual favours.'

The lift doors opened.

Tahlia stepped forward. 'You don't have to assure *me* anything, despite your lack of assistant,' she shot over her shoulder.

He wanted to assure her of so many things, but the scars still ached from Celia. 'Well, that's the thing,' he said slowly, following her. 'Until I get one, I'll need some help.'

She swung to face him. 'Of course. You've met quite a few of the staff. Have you anyone in mind…maybe from the copy room or mail room on a temporary basis?' She touched a flushed cheek; her nails, long and rounded, were painted the same peach as her lips. 'Until we get someone else in, you know, advertising and interviews take time.'

Case shrugged, slipping his hands deep into his trouser pockets. 'I'm thinking of someone who's very aware of who's who and what's what and how the place is run.'

She looked towards her office, pointing in that direction, avoiding his gaze. 'Great. Look, I'd love to chat on and on but I do have work to do, as you well know. And I'm sure you do too. Having such a senior position and all. If that's all? Let me know what you decide…how you want to do it…*who.*'

Case rocked back on his heels, taking in her tall, shapely body, her neat black skirt and jacket, her white sleeveless shirt. Her all-business appearance covering the all-enticing challenge that gleamed in her eyes like burning embers waiting for his breath.

He knew exactly who he wanted. 'Actually, I'm thinking of you.'

CHAPTER SEVEN

'What does not destroy me, makes me stronger.'
Yeah, right, Nietzsche. *And who does not drive you crazy, can't steal your job and make you act stupid?*

TAHLIA sat at her desk, staring at her computer screen. Case *Taunting* Darrington couldn't mean *her*, want her, as his assistant—that was just wrong, humiliating and wrong, and stirring and sexy and wrong.

As if she was going to accept a job helping out the competition, the man who had stolen her job, her promotion, her rise, her nice safe rung that she was going to conduct the next challenge of her life from.

Hell, the man had taken so much from her he didn't deserve anything but the same confusion and pain he was putting her through.

This was her life he was messing up, her feelings he was messing with and her anchor he'd cut loose with no concern for the weather.

She gripped the desk tightly. Just because her life was fraying at the edges didn't mean she didn't have her act together and couldn't handle anything that came her way…no matter who her father was or what he'd done.

Tahlia lifted her chin and clicked on her inbox.

TO: *TahliaM@WWWDesigns.com*
CC: *KeelyR@WWWDesigns.com*

FROM: *EmmaR@WWWDesigns.com*
RE: SOS

Still okay for tonight? Can't wait to hear about your mysterious SOS.

I'll bring a couple of my favourite romantic movies to soothe your soul. And chokkies.

Have you seen Chrystal? She's acting weird and standing in quiet corners with the pot plants. It's truly freaky. Do you know what's going on?

Em

Tahlia sighed. Chrystal was the last thing on her mind. She wasn't just the office date-a-holic, she was the resident drama-queen.

As one of the receptionists-cum-fix-it gals Chrystal was all over the place. It could be anything or anyone that had disturbed Chrystal, from a new male in the building to a new female too-good-looking for her comfort to a resident female wearing the same outfit, jewellery or shoes.

Tahlia's only surprise was that they all hadn't heard the latest development in Chrystal's life firsthand, at least twice.

Actually, she wouldn't mind listening to one of Chrystal's adventures rather than dwelling on Case Darrington.

TO: *TahliaM@WWWDesigns.com*
CC: *EmmaR@WWWDesigns.com*
FROM: *KeelyR@WWWDesigns.com*
RE: SOS

You can count on me being there too. The SOS
sounds very mysterious. And I'm coming with
wine—to enjoy vicariously through my mates—and
doughnuts!

Re Chrystal: Do you think it could be Liam, that shy
programmer downstairs, who's caught her eye finally? Sure, he's nothing like Chrystal. He's as shy
as a monk and as nerdy as hell. But he's cute and
he must be the only fresh meat left.

She's had to have done every single straight guy in
the place, and then some. Except Liam and
Darrington, but he's way out of her league. Tahlia,
is he married? I heard you two had lunch—is he the
reason for the SOS?

See you tonight where you must tell all!

Keely

Tahlia stared at her screen. She'd love to tell all, but
she wasn't sure she could tell her friends anything if
she wasn't sure what was going on, least of all with
herself.

Where was her usual together self? Would her
friends even recognise this babbling bimbo she'd
turned into and help her resolve her current angst?

Should she even try or, as her mother said, deal with
it on her own because the challenges in life were to
make *us* grow, not to leech off or lean on others?

She scrolled through her inbox of business memos.
At least her friends would help her wipe her mind of
every annoying trace of Case *Taxing* Darrington with
their movies, their treats and their company.

Maybe she shouldn't have invited them. How would

she survive hours with them and not blurt out her incredibly stupid attraction to Darrington, despite his
snobby-arrogant-potential-playboy-jerkdom?   They'd
think she was an idiot.

Maybe she could distract them by getting them to
help with her criteria for a partner instead, to narrow
down her prospects, help her pick the qualities in a man
that she could live with for the rest of her life.

Tahlia snatched up a pen. She wasn't about to get
into dating without a plan. She didn't want to be re-
sponsible for hurt feelings, crushed dreams or unreal
expectations. She didn't want to be anybody's last
straw.

She closed her eyes against the wave of memories
that crashed against her heart. How had her mother
picked herself up, carrying all those burdens, after her
father had died?

Had she been haunted by questions, wondering what
it had been that broke her husband's will to live? Had
she been tortured by their last argument over unpaid
bills, her need for him to be there for her, for him to
be a good father?

Had she wished she could take back her last words,
the last time she saw him, time itself? Tahlia's throat
tightened. Like she did.

She jerked straight-backed, blinking away the ache,
and picked up a file and flipped it open. Business was
safer to think about, deal with and be involved in than
all that personal stuff, except where Darrington was
concerned.

She chewed on her bottom lip. She didn't like being

as out of control as she was around Case Darrington, and feeling way too much.

It just wasn't professional and the sooner he was gone the better. And if she had to be the one to show him the door, so be it.

It would be a giant step in the right direction.

Case dropped his attaché case and knelt down on the polished timber floor and hugged Edison, nestling his face in his neck, breathing in his heavy doggy scent in an effort to douse the haunting memory of Tahlia's perfume.

'Hey Edi, you miss me, boy?' he crooned, slapping Edi's back and standing up, loosening his tie and kicking off his shoes. 'It's been one hell of a day.'

He'd driven himself insane all afternoon, trying to rationalise his impromptu request for Tahlia to be his assistant. Was it logical or a knee-jerk reaction to her story about the last Marketing Executive?

Running into that Chrystal woman in the lift again had just topped off his agony. At least they hadn't been alone, but that hadn't seemed to deter her.

Evading her probing, very personal questions had been one challenge, avoiding her pushing herself up against him a whole other dilemma.

Case shrugged off his suit jacket and tossed it over the black leather recliner. He was supposed to be the Marketing Executive, not some mouse for the woman to toy with. Hell, if she only knew who he really was!

One thing he was going to outlaw was desperate women. They freaked him out.

'That you, Mr Darrington, sir?' Luciana's heavy accent laced every word and echoed around the high ceilings of his open-plan loft-style apartment.

The designer had got a bit carried away with the stream running down the hallway under glass and the waterfall in the lounge, but Edi didn't seem to mind it. Better than the toilet bowl.

His Italian house-fairy heaved her ample frame from the hallway that accessed the laundry room and kitchen, wiping her hands on her canary-yellow apron. 'Dinner is in oven. Timer dings, you eat. Yes?'

'Yes, thank you,' he said, smiling at the woman who liked to think she'd adopted him. He couldn't live without her. She cleaned the house, cooked and kept Edison company while he wasn't around. He should have discovered his housekeeper phenomenon before he married Celia; he may have decided he didn't need the anguish.

Luciana snatched up a heavy cane bag from the floor, beside the black steel and smoked glass dining table, shoved her apron deep inside and straightened the greying coil of hair at her nape. 'You good boy. Nice boy. You need good woman.'

He shrugged. It was a familiar conversation he had with her, and a sure-fire way of having all the single young females of her family tree described to him. 'I have you.'

She laughed. 'I help you find,' she sang, opening the front door, pausing, taking out a cloth from her bag and wiping down the ochre wall beside her. 'If you not finding.'

'I don't need help, but thank you anyway, Luciana,' he said, lurching forward and ushering the most valuable employee he had to the lift. He punched the button. 'See you tomorrow?'

The doors opened. She stepped in and turned. 'Yes. What you want for dinner? I could cook special lasagne, secret recipe?' she said, eyeing him carefully.

Case could read the gleam in her eyes. Probably lining up a whole meal that she planned him to share with someone she knew.

'No dinner. I have a date,' he rushed on. Better to eat out alone than endure Luciana's umpteen single relatives' profiles again and be asked to pick one. Maybe Simon would be free.

She nodded, her smile wide. 'Good. You need a good woman.'

The doors closed and he wandered back to his penthouse suite, closing the double doors behind him and looking out of the floor-to-ceiling glass windows that stretched the entire wall at the view of the northern shore of the bay.

He didn't need any help in finding a woman. He found plenty. Finding one who liked him for who he was…was the hard part. Who wanted to know him, be with him, for him.

How to find said woman was the biggest dilemma in his life. He couldn't help but question a woman's motives if she knew all he had. He wondered how he'd broach protecting his assets from another bad choice, how he could downplay his portfolio and try to assess whether it was him she liked or his money.

The phone rang and Case answered.

'So what was with today?' Simon asked in his best

lawyer-cum-best-mate tone of inquisition. 'A desire to play undercover agent?'

'A desire to make everything I own into a resounding success, actually,' Case stated drily. And he sure needed the challenge of taking his newest acquisition back into the black.

He had needed to distract him from himself. 'I was out with my Director of Sales.' And her very fine green eyes.

'Why didn't you just go there—no lies? You *are* the new owner of WWW Designs.'

Case sank into a recliner chair. 'Because of all the airs and graces that are always put on to muddy the truth.'

He'd already seen the myriad attempts of the General Manager at WWW Designs to flatter him into keeping her on; the woman was practically dripping with greasy compliments—on his clothes, his business acumen and his plan to be put on the staff incognito.

Case knew the best way to maximize the company's efficiency was to get in there and see how it was being run firsthand and nothing was going to stop him, especially a small thing like a few white lies. The fact that he needed to escape the monotony of his routine didn't come into it. Much.

'So you're after the truth by telling lies.' Simon made a guttural noise deep in his throat. 'You know you don't have to keep on with it—you could get someone else to do it.'

Case loosened his tie. 'No. I like it there.' And liked being surprised by a certain member of his staff and her lack of hesitation in speaking her mind.

Simon groaned. 'Come on, get serious. Your time is far too valuable to put into this. Just employ an efficiency expert, or *I* could go.'

Case rubbed his smooth jaw, loath to put words to the hollow feeling in his chest at the thought of backing down from this challenge. 'I don't see it that way.' This was an opportunity just begging for him to conquer it…and maybe, hopefully, fill that void for just a little while.

And what a challenge. WWW Designs was the biggest firm of its type in the state and he was itching to turn the company around and shove its success in all the biggest rags and in a few faces who had failed to see how much more he was than just a suit and a bank balance.

'What about the ethics of it?'

Case smiled. 'What ethics would they be? As the new owner I could have sacked them all but I'd rather find out how they're doing things and where the problems lie. I'd hate to get rid of valuable staff.'

'Right, sure, that's what it is. And the fact that you were getting bored doesn't come into it?'

Case stared at the modern painting on the wall. Simon was too smart. 'Okay, I admit it. I wanted to do something new. There's no crime in that. I'm sure you're holding the fort.'

He was so sick of presiding over a clockwork company, being obliged to attend one function after another and kissing arse to every prestigious alliance in the business.

'Sure, I can take care of the company, if I can call you to make the decisions without using some damned code.' Simon cleared his throat. 'But come on, be serious, what are you expecting to find there?'

'I'm looking…' Case rubbed Edi's chin with his foot '…for something…' To wipe out the empty feeling that had been eating him up inside. Ignoring it hadn't helped. Dating hadn't helped. Work hadn't even helped, until now.

'Well, I can tell you you're not going to find it at WWW Designs. But are you sure about what you're getting yourself into?'

'Not a problem; nothing there that I can't handle.' Case rang off, Tahlia Moran's sweet face coming to his mind.

Tahlia Moran didn't know what he had, the companies he owned, the properties that were his, the people that he rubbed shoulders with or the five cars parked downstairs in the garage.

She hadn't questioned him on choosing companies to buy out today at lunch—had probably accepted that he was playing the stock market, not playing Monopoly.

Was this his chance?

She was all he could think about since lunch, and he'd acted impulsively. He'd made that reckless phone call before leaving work. The one that had tortured him all the way home.

It was way too early for gestures like that.

Hell, was he being silly entertaining the thought that he could have a relationship with the woman? Could he be incensed by lust into making another mistake that could not only cost him dearly, but break what was left of his heart?

The trouble was that she was incredible. A man didn't meet incredible often in his life... How could he ignore incredible?

Edi sat by his feet, his tail pounding the floor.

Case glanced down at the big dark eyes of his best friend and companion. 'I'm being an idiot, aren't I? Getting carried away, just because I feel something more than what I normally feel. It's nothing, right?'

Edi's tongue lolled out of his mouth.

'Time for a walk, hey?'

He knew exactly what he had to do. Stay away from the incredible woman, at least while he had a job to do that involved being near her.

He could plead ignorance if she mentioned his brash action... What had he been thinking? He knew more than anyone that nothing could be built on lies.

Case hauled himself up out of his chair. Maybe she wouldn't even guess it was from him. She probably had a heap of men in her life anyway. A woman that beautiful...

Case raked both hands through his hair and back over his face, slapping himself on the cheeks. This thing between them was probably nothing anyway.

Staying away would prove that his attraction was nothing more than convenience, just because Tahlia and her hot body and fiery eyes were there, and nothing more.

How hard could it be to avoid her?

She wasn't about to take up his incredibly rash invitation to be his assistant...and he'd be flat out assessing employee performance, sifting through personnel files and meeting them all, one by one. And it was a big office.

Case swung around, striding to the hallstand and taking out the leash. Edi followed, his tongue wagging, panting his eagerness.

There was no reason to see her at all.

CHAPTER EIGHT

What I want in a man on a good day:
1) Tall, dark and reasonably good-looking
2) White collar professional
3) Sense of humour
4) Reasonably sane in-laws
What I want in a man on a bad day: space

'YES, Mum. I am looking after myself.' Tahlia threw herself on to the couch, a nuked bowl of low-fat noodle dish in one hand and the phone in the other.

'And the promotion?'

She stared at the ceiling. 'No news yet.' There was no way she was going there with her mother, least of all admitting how the new guy had not only taken her job but had turned her world inside out and wanted her to be his assistant—glorified or not. Her mother would go nuts.

Her mother figured Tahlia had her life together, under control and on plan like hers was. Usually, she'd be right. Today she was so far from it, it made Tahlia's belly fight the noodles.

She couldn't tell her.

Her mother would demand the entire story and every detail so she could bestow her wisdom and advice to remedy the problem.

Tahlia was used to it. As a child she'd listened with

her mother to motivational tapes, had filled out goal
sheets and dream journals and said affirmations just
like her mum.

She knew the drill and knew exactly what her mother
would say and she couldn't bring herself to share the
sorry news and hear the disappointment in her mother's
voice.

She'd tortured herself enough for one day with
Case's request to be his assistant.

Maybe it was just another way to torture her into
submission. Damn the man. Wasn't it enough that she
was tortured by his smile, his eyes, his very fine-
looking body? And thoughts of him being all too human with his shaggy little dog and all.

'I'll let you know—' she said carefully, watching her
tone.

Her mother tsked. 'Still nothing? And you're home
this early? Couldn't you have found something to do
at the office to show them that you're keen?'

Tahlia sighed, pushing the red velvet cushions
around beside her. 'I have been, Mum. But I do have
to have a life too.'

She took a mouthful of noodles, staring at the news-
caster on the muted TV in the corner, the pile of business management books on her coffee table and the
fashion magazine laid open to the latest in-office wear
for kick-arse professional women.

'Are you sure you've done everything you can to
make your boss see your assets?'

'Yes, Mum.' Tahlia couldn't help but smile. Her new
boss seemed very aware of her assets…and the thought

of his blue gaze coursing over her body made her nerves tingle anew.

There was a long pause. 'Are you dating?' her mother asked in a whole different are-you-running-your-life-right? tone.

Tahlia swallowed the lump of food that threatened to choke her, putting the bowl on the coffee table beside the wineglasses and empty bowls set out for the girls. 'Dating the boss?' She coughed. 'No. Of course not.'

'I meant dating in general, honey. Of course you're not dating your boss.'

Tahlia shook herself. 'Right.' Of course the thought hadn't crossed her mind; it probably hadn't even crossed Case Darrington's.

'You know you shouldn't let anything distract you from what really matters.'

'Yes, Mum. I know.'

'You know the risks involved in relationships, how messy they can be…' Her mother sighed heavily. 'You know how important it is to get your life right first.'

'Yes, Mum. I'm getting that promotion first, Mum.'

'That's a good girl. I'm so happy that you're learning from my mistakes and you don't have to go through what I—'

Tahlia cringed. 'Yes. I'm so lucky to have you.' There were some lessons she could do without, even if it meant settling for someone safe rather than someone who was trouble. 'And don't worry, I will get that promotion.'

'Of course you will.'

She shifted in her seat. Some time, after she figured

out where Darrington came from and what he was up
to. 'Look, I have to go. My dinner's getting cold and
I have a ton of work in front of me.'

'That's the girl,' her mother gushed. 'You make it
so they can't do anything but give you the promotion.
You just have to do more. Bye now.'

Tahlia rang off, a cold ache in her chest. She *had*
thought she'd done everything, but obviously it wasn't
enough. Yet.

One thing was for sure; Raquel couldn't help but
notice soon that Darrington wasn't getting the job
done—he was spending far too much energy on the
staff and neglecting the rest of his work.

All she needed to do was wait…

She gave her neat apartment a slow assessment. She
had only one bedroom to minimise rental costs and
maximise her saving capability, a small kitchen to
make her own food rather than rely on take-aways, a
large fridge full of water, fruit and vegetables and frozen meals for one.

It was all about moderation. Why hadn't her father
seen it? Moderation and control was the key to life. If
he'd mastered it he wouldn't have needed to have lied
to her mother about the poor state of business, their
financial difficulty and his state of mind.

He wouldn't have needed time to himself so much,
wouldn't have drunk so much and wouldn't have been
on the balcony that night…wouldn't have leant so
heavily on that loose rail.

Sirens still made her body chill and every part of her
freeze and listen, for the sound of her mother talking
with her father at the table as though he was there, safe,

as though they were there, together, as though life was all okay again and her father hadn't fallen to his death leaving all those problems they said he couldn't face for her mother.

The doorbell rang.

She put down her bowl and strode to the door. At last. Her friends. She couldn't have done with her own company a moment longer, especially when her mind was filled with images of Case and his wide shoulders, slim hips, cute tight butt and those incredible sapphire-blue eyes.

She swung the door wide.

Roses. Plump crimson blooms filled the doorway, with soft sprays of baby's breath at the edges and deep green leaves intermingled amongst the rich vivid flowers in front of her.

She froze, her breath stuck in her throat. Was Case on the other side of the veritable garden? Were his eyes going to be sparkling with promises his lips couldn't wait to fulfil, his blood rushing as fiery hot as the colour of the roses, just waiting to sweep her to him…?

The flowers moved aside. 'For Miss Moran,' said the delivery man, thrusting a clipboard under her nose for her to sign, his face beaming as though he was giving them to her himself.

The chill of reality cooled her body.

Idiot. As if he'd come over. Sure, the guy looked at her and was nice but it didn't mean anything except that it had been far too long since she'd been on a date.

He was her boss! As if the guy was going to send her flowers—but if not him, then who?

She signed and gave the man his pen and board

back. Why had she neglected her personal life so badly? If she hadn't she wouldn't be so at a loss every time she was in the vicinity of Case.

If she was a dating veteran she probably wouldn't even register Case and his attributes, she'd be used to men and attention and wouldn't be tortured thinking about a man so obviously unsuitable for her.

Tahlia took the roses and held them close to her chest, breathing in their sweet scent. Nice. She hadn't had roses since…too long.

It was a lovely thought. Her mother? No way. Emma and Keely, maybe…

She closed the front door, flipping open the card tucked amongst the stems. *'Thinking of you.'*

Case, or a secret admirer? 'Yeah, right.' It had to be him. Logic suggested there were no other viable options for the sender. *He liked her.*

She closed her eyes and let the realisation wash over her. Did he want to get to know her better?

The thought wasn't entirely unattractive, especially the part where she and Case would be in each other's arms, tasting each other's lips, their bodies pressed together, exploring the amazing chemistry that was making her act insane.

Was life about compromise?

She glanced at Bert and Ernie. She could put a glass lid on top of their fish bowl and get that pussycat that her mother had never let her have.

No.

She held the bunch of flowers away from her, shaking her head. She was not going to waste valuable time with stupid fantasies about the boss.

She was not going to entertain thoughts like that about the man who stole her job, flowers or not.

She was *not* giving up. She was a professional and that was *her* promotion, no matter what he made her feel.

The doorbell rang again.

She flung open the door, steeling herself. If Case Darrington thought that a bunch of flowers was going to romance her into his way of thinking…

Emma and Keely filled the doorway. 'We're here.'

They bustled in, arms full of bags, the pizza wafting cheesy garlic aromas around the room.

'Who's your admirer?' Keely asked.

Tahlia tossed the flowers on to the hallstand. 'Work…from work. Condolences on my promotionless week.'

Emma picked up the flowers, cradling them in her arms. 'We should have thought of that. Who did?' She plucked the card. 'Who's thinking of you?'

'Raquel,' Tahlia blurted.

'Yeah, that you're not breathing down her neck. Two-faced Rottie that she is.' Keely drew her into a hug, juggling pizza and packages. 'She should have given you the job, not that jerk.'

Emma waved the card. 'Hang on. How dumb do you think we are? Raquel wouldn't spend a dime on sending you anything, let alone flowers.' Emma took the flowers into the kitchen. 'Fess up.'

'Fine.' Tahlia slipped the pizza from Keely's hands, strode into the lounge, dropped into her favourite deep-cushioned chair and opened the box. 'I'm pretty sure they're from Case Darrington.'

Emma whistled, pulling a vase out of the cupboard below the sink and filling it with water. 'He is rather cute and if I didn't have my wonderful Harry I would consider pushing him into a cupboard and ripping his clothes off.'

Tahlia stared at her friend, trying not to let the image infect her, her stomach holding on to the thought and pushing it low.

'And?' Emma unwrapped the bunch and slid the stalks into the vase. 'He glanced across the crowded office,' she said dreamily. 'Saw you standing there with your freshly pressed jacket, white shirt that struggled to contain your throbbing heart and a short skirt show-ing off long, long freshly waxed legs that he couldn't wait to have wrapped around him—'

'No,' Tahlia snapped, pushing down the heat in her veins. That girl had been watching too many romances.

She looked away. She couldn't tell them everything now and confess what she was feeling. It was just too embarrassing. 'Not exactly. I think he's an ass. A jerk. An office playboy just toying with me.' She shook her head with vigour. 'I don't want to talk about him.'

'Okay,' Emma said, stifling a smile, whipping her fingers across her lips. 'No more talk about the play-boy.'

'All right.' Keely nestled herself on the sofa. 'But then what was the SOS for?'

'I need help…with my list for my perfect man,' she rushed on. As if that would ever happen. 'Like you had, Keely. I figure if I had a checklist I think I may be better equipped to find someone to settle down with.' Somewhere in the distant future.

Emma placed the vase of roses on the hallstand. 'Really. Truly? You're finally going to do it? Even without the promotion?'

Tahlia cringed. There was no way, but she had to get them off the promotion and Case subject. 'I know I've used that job as an excuse not to get into dating and maybe I used it a bit much. You know, all those eggs in one basket thing. I think I need to work on another basket while I mop up the broken eggs in my other one.'

'Sure. I get it.' Keely nodded slowly. 'You need time to grieve…and all. What have you got so far?'

Tahlia pulled out the scrap of paper she'd been doodling on this week, paused and folded it, tucking it tight under her thigh. It was already all wrong.

She ripped open a pack of M&Ms Keely had unpacked on to the table and tipped them into a bowl, snagging a couple of strays and popping them into her mouth. 'I haven't got much so far. Short, blond and…' Not handsome. She'd had enough of handsome. 'I don't mind if he's had a close encounter with a brick wall.'

Tahlia scooped a large handful of M&Ms into her lap and leant back, tucking her legs up on to the seat. 'I think that sort of broken nose, scarred face, thinning hair sort of look is one that screams character,' she blurted, shoving half of the load into her mouth.

Emma flopped on to the sofa, ripping open a bag of sweets, shooting Keely a look. 'And his job?'

Tahlia chewed hard and swallowed. 'His job—something where he gets down and dirty.' She rushed on, trying to rid pastel shirts and silk ties from haunting her mind. 'None of this intellectual shirty-suited sort of person. I want someone rugged, calloused and… rugged.'

Tahlia took a breath and shoved the rest of the M&Ms in her mouth, glancing to the bottle on the table, crunching them up. She needed something stronger than sweets…

Emma popped the cork on the wine, grabbing a slice of the cheesy pizza. 'And this man's hobbies would be—?'

'Collecting bottle tops maybe, tattoos or beer bottles or sandals lost on the beach,' Tahlia said in a rush. There. As totally opposite to *that* man as she could possibly get. 'Well? What do you think?'

'I think you'll find him at the local pub, swilling down beer and chewing glass.' Keely laughed. 'Are you setting yourself up for disappointment or just afraid of dating?'

Tahlia jerked to her feet. She didn't like where this was going. She wasn't afraid of dating or men, not in general anyway. 'No. I'm being practical.'

Emma poured a glass and slid it in front of Tahlia and picked up a pen. 'Right. I think you ought to start fresh. What have you got—?' She lurched forward and snatched the piece of paper from her chair. 'This is more like it. What's wrong with this tall, dark and handsome white-collar intellectual—? Oh.'

'What oh?' Keely leaned forward, holding her stomach. 'What have I missed?'

Finishing off her slice of pizza, Emma opened a bag of popcorn, balancing it on her lap and waved the paper

at her. 'I think our Tahlia has already fallen for someone but is in denial.'

Tahlia slumped back into her seat and crossed her
arms. 'I'm denying nothing.' And she wasn't admitting
anything either. 'I have not fallen for anyone. I do not
fall. I make lists and plans and stay aware of all con-
tingencies at all times.'

Emma tossed a piece of popcorn at her. 'Right. Sure.
Liar.'

'I'm not lying. There is no way I'm interested in
Case Darrington as anything other than my arch nem-
esis that I need to crush like a bug.'

'That doesn't sound healthy.' Keely poured cola into
her glass.

'You should have heard him. He expected me to be
his assistant until he hired someone. Me!' She touched
her chest, feeling the rage anew. It felt far safer than
those other feelings she didn't want to have. 'After he
had the nerve to steal my promotion, he wants to make
me his assistant.'

Emma tipped the popcorn into a bowl and pulled out
some more packages. 'Sweetie, take the job, play the
secretary-cum-assistant role—it would be great for you
to get to know him, wouldn't it?'

'You guys are crazy.'

'Go on, email him now and tell him you'll help him
out with the job. It doesn't have to be for long.' Emma
took another slice of pizza. 'It will resolve, once and
for all, whether it's displaced animosity that you feel
for your new boss, lust or something else entirely…'

Keely waved a chocolate-covered jam doughnut.
'And thank him for the flowers.'

'And you could tell him you're thinking of him too,' Emma lilted, casting her gaze to the incredible bunch of red roses on the hallstand.

She was, but she wasn't thinking straight. She was considering her friends' advice, but sense would suggest it was extremely flawed and terribly biased in favour of her associating with a cute-suit instead of focusing on her career.

Could these strong feelings be caused by her anger? She nodded. Definitely…it made far more sense than considering she'd let anyone touch her heart, let alone someone who'd taken something so precious from her, or someone who could make her feel so vulnerable.

That had to be wrong.

Tahlia took her glass. Maybe she *could* spend some more time with the boss, get beneath that tailored exterior of his, past the sweet soppy dog-at-home thing and reveal the true jerk underneath.

Tahlia knocked back her wine and settled back into her chair with a slice of pizza in one hand and an iced doughnut in the other. She'd give the matter some serious thought and maybe check out her horoscope in the morning to see if the stars could shed anything on the matter.

She bit into the sweet powdery softness of the doughnut. One thing she did know was that she was not going to rush into anything, least of all him.

CHAPTER NINE

***They say all things good to
know are difficult to learn.***
*Especially when it involves alcohol, romantic
movies, too much sugar and way too helpful friends.*

TAHLIA strode through the foyer, every step a challenge to the fragile head on her shoulders that still didn't feel like her own.

They'd drunk far too much on Friday night, or at least *she* had, but she was sure they'd all be suffering the morning-afters for days.

Keely had polished off every last doughnut, citing the extra mouth she had to feed, and Emma's chocolate consumption would've put a ten-year-old to shame.

Tahlia had spent most of the weekend tucked up in bed with the weekend papers and the *Business Review*, nursing her hangover, her promotion failure and an addled brain full of Darrington fantasies.

Why had she drunk so much?

She waved to George, tucking the newspaper tighter under her arm. She'd deliberately avoided reading her horoscope this morning because she didn't want to know, and especially didn't want to be tempted to check for what Sagittarians were up to today—as if she cared. Did it matter what Case's was? It did not.

Sure, she'd emailed him under the influence some

time in the wee hours of Friday night, taking up the offer to be his assistant, but it didn't have to be the disaster she'd first thought it was when she'd realised what she'd done.

Sure, she'd let herself get talked into it by Emma and Keely, but after two days analysing the pros and cons she had to say it was the right thing to do.

There were too many question marks around Darrington. It was time to resolve some of them, once and for all, and spending time in close proximity seemed a perfect opportunity to do just that.

He was up to something, she was sure of it.

She was a professional, after all. What could it hurt to take the opportunity to see just what he was up to and harden her heart to feeling anything for the man?

So he had probably sent her the flowers. It didn't mean anything, except that he was looking for more distractions from doing the job.

Marketing Executives weren't usually so obsessed with the staff right down to the copy kids temping while in uni, let alone the mail clerks.

She had to find out what Case Darrington was about, then expose his failings to Raquel and get the job that should have been hers in the first place.

Her fantasies would be squashed, thankfully—they were taking too much of her time, torturing her with memories of imagined glances, warm smiles and soft words that couldn't possibly exist anywhere except in her addled brain. And in unexplainable flower deliveries.

She punched the lift button.

'Good morning, Tahlia.' A familiar nasal bark.

Tahlia turned to look Raquel Wilson in the eye. She was the same height as Tahlia but solid, wearing crimson trousers with hot red stilettos and a black cotton top that clung to her like a second skin.

'I'm sorry you had to find out about the position of Marketing Executive the way you did.'

Sure she was. Tahlia forced herself to keep a straight face, to keep the raging heat churning up inside from bursting from her mouth. The Rottie's cool regard for Tahlia when she was just another employee had turned to chilling after she'd become Director of Sales.

Raquel waved her Rolex-clad arm, her diamond rings glinting. 'I know how much you wanted the job.'

'Yes,' she said and shrugged. Best to pretend it didn't matter than admit weakness in the face of power personified. Raquel could rip her throat out professionally, if given half a chance and even less of an excuse.

Raquel forced a laugh as fake as her nose. 'Just wanted to clear the air between us so there's no hard feelings.'

Tahlia nodded. 'Right. Sure.' As if. The woman was paranoid about Tahlia's slow and steady climb up the corporate ladder.

'I'd hate for you to take being overlooked for the promotion personally.' Raquel tossed her jet-black dyed hair back from her shoulder. 'And I really don't have much time spare to write you out a reference, but if you insist…'

'No. I'm not taking it personally at all.' She forced a smile. If only Raquel knew just how personal the whole thing was getting, the scent of the roses coming

back to her, with a pair of sapphire-blue eyes that
turned her world upside down.

She took a slow breath. 'I'm sure your decision was
taken with the utmost care and Mr Darrington is *far*
more qualified for the position than me.' At least as far
as Raquel had been concerned at the time, but showing
her how wrong she was would be incredibly satisfying.
'Where on earth did you find him?'

Raquel's grin faded. 'Oh, around.'

Tahlia raised her eyebrows—the Rottie had to guess
she'd put the wrong person in the job. 'And around
would be?'

Raquel's eyes narrowed. 'Well…look, sometimes
the best people come through unexpected channels.'
She stepped towards the doors. 'You understand?'

'I think I do,' Tahlia said slowly, her mind churning.

The doors opened and Raquel alighted. 'You will be
nice to the man, won't you?' she tossed back at her.
'He is new and isn't familiar with the job and its re-
quirements and will need all the guidance and assis-
tance that you can offer him.'

Tahlia gave a light shrug. 'Of course,' she said
strongly, gritting her teeth. She couldn't wait to help
him do the job he had been hired for.

The doors started to close.

'I'd expect nothing less from you,' the Rottie shot
back.

Tahlia stared after the big boss, every part of her
wanting to scream, yell and cry at the injustice. She
took a deep breath, willing her blood to cool.

She was in control. So the man *had* got her promotion on the sly. She'd damned well be *his* assistant
and give him the helping hand he needed, right out the
door.

CHAPTER TEN

Keep your friends close and your enemy—
Case Taker *Darrington closer still—as close as I can*
handle…and more. I'm going to know more about his
skeletons than my own and then I'm going to bury him.

TAHLIA dropped into the desk outside Case's office.
Getting romanced out of a job sucked, Case expecting
her to be romanced into being his secretary was a joke,
and she was all for making hers the last laugh.

She was so going to prove her point, no matter what
small furry animals the guy had at home.

Tahlia stabbed the keyboard.

> TO: *EmmaR@WWWDesigns.com*
> CC: *KeelyR@WWWDesigns.com*
> FROM: *TahliaM@WWWDesigns.com*
> RE: Men

You two were wrong. Looks like Case *Treacherous*
Darrington is a jerk. Just spoke to Raquel, who ex-
pects me to babysit the guy into being a competent
Exec in lieu of me. Sounds like no experience and
potential leech. Crap.

Life sucks.

Keely, sure, Liam is cute and shy and looks at
Chrystal a lot but could it be possible that she could
be interested in a real relationship?

No, Case is not married. No girlfriend, but I'd say
he's had quite a few. Not that I care.
And no, don't you two start on this stupid attraction
thing again—it absolutely does not exist.
Have to go through being his PA thanks to two particular sugar-inebriated friends and emailing under
the influence.
I tell you this interaction with this sub-human job-
stealer is for the good of the company and all aspir-
ing employees everywhere, nothing personal.
T

Tahlia stared at his office door. She'd yet to knock
and tell the guy just how personal this wasn't.

She stood up slowly. He was trouble to her and the
company and it was her duty to sort him out before he
caused any damage to the already-hampered WWW.

She needed to find out more about him, and straight
from the source. She had to get the guy to lighten up,
to open up, to reveal his secrets.

Tahlia had got some advice, in a roundabout way so
as not to highlight her goal. Keely had suggested beer
to get a guy to open up. Em, being Em, had suggested
seduction.

Against her better judgement but for the good of the
company, she'd decided to act nice and flirt the guy
into dropping his guard.

If he could use his connections to procure her promotion, she could use her God-given wiles to get what
she needed.

Her blood fired at the thought of playing with the
fire in Case's eyes.

She smoothed down her jacket. For the future of WWW Designs, home to her friends and many a talented person who deserved a far better boss, she'd make the sacrifice.

She owed it that.

TO: *TahliaM@WWWDesigns.com*
CC: *EmmaR@WWWDesigns.com*
FROM: *KeelyR@WWWDesigns.com*
RE: Men

I think you protest too much, honey.

And Chrystal wanting a relationship? Why not? She's human, isn't she? I think eventually we all need something more in our lives. And I'm so glad I've found it.

K

Well, bully for her.

Tahlia pushed away from the desk and rapped on Case *Test-time* Darrington's door and swung it wide. 'Good morning, Mr Darrington.'

'Tahlia,' he offered, smoothly rising. 'I got your message. I…I was surprised, to say the least…'

Case wasn't wearing his suit jacket, just a baby-blue shirt sitting as enticingly around those wide shoulders as his tailored jacket had been. His trousers were dark and his deep aqua silk tie brought out flecks of dazzling light in his eyes.

Gawd, he looked good. Too good. She shifted on her black heels. 'Me, too. Surprised, that is.' At the roses, at herself, at her email accepting this assistant job and at her tenacity.

He shot her a sheepish grin. 'I figured you'd think it was below you…'

'Not at all,' she said smoothly, flicking her fringe back. 'You're my boss and I'm quite happy to do whatever you feel best serves the company.'

'Yes, well…'

She stepped forward, her fingers flexing, a crazy desire to run her hand over his smooth clean jaw rushing through her. 'And thank you for the flowers.'

'Flowers? Me?' He cast a look to the windows. 'Sorry, I don't know anything about flowers.'

Tahlia paused. 'You didn't send the flowers?'

'Look, about you being my assistant—'

Didn't he still want her as his assistant? Didn't he want to admit he had the finest taste in roses? Or that he'd been thinking of her…?

'Is there something wrong?' she asked slowly, trying to make him out—just standing there looking incredibly gorgeous. His blue gaze pinned her to the spot, making her heart clatter in her chest. 'I can procure you a secretary from somewhere else in the office if you think I'm unsuitable in any way,' she said in a rush, running through the possibilities of stealing someone from somewhere for him if that was what he wanted.

Case stood immobile, his brow furrowed as though he was having some war of his own.

Tahlia flicked back her fringe, standing taller. What was she thinking? *She* had to do this. It didn't matter how cute or hot or serious he looked. 'But I do think that *your* idea of me helping you out and acclimatising you to the office is a great one. Save you a lot of time and it's not like it has to be for ever, just a few days or so. I can help you out and do my job, just from the desk here.' She jabbed her thumb behind her.

That should be enough. It wasn't as if he would pose much of a challenge, not when he was looking at her like that, running his gaze down her black trouser suit that was tailored perfectly around the soft curves of her hips, the jacket contoured perfectly to shape her waist, the lapels small but angled low, highlighting the lace chemise-like top she wore like a shirt and the view of the valley of her breasts it afforded.

It was a great choice for suggesting a softer, gentler side, a side that was all ears to whatever he wanted to share.

'Great. I'm glad you agree…' He ran a hand through his hair, pulling his gaze to her face and her Peach Passion lips '…with my idea. That's great… I'm sure this will be great. Thanks.'

She sauntered to the chair by the wall, gripping the back tightly, avoiding the windows. How long would she have to endure this extreme torture at the mercy of those incredible blue eyes and deep voice and steamy looks?

Tahlia slid on to the chair, crossing her legs carefully. 'So where do we start?' she said softly.

Case sat down, holding his hands tightly in front of him. 'How about we start with you? How about you tell me a little about your history, your aspirations and what the company needs to do to help you fulfil those goals?'

'My goals?' She couldn't help but stare at the guy in the big black leather chair that was going to be hers, the office that ought to have her name on it, the walls she was going to hang her photos and qualifications on and the bank of windows that she'd been ready to hang vertical blinds on. What could she say?

He leant forward, his eyebrows rising slightly. 'You do have goals?'

'Of course I have goals,' she bit out. How dared he? 'I've had goals since I was twelve, when I decided I was going to run a kick-arse company like this one, and not for one minute have I ever questioned that I was going to make it. My aspirations? To sit at the head of this company and run it properly and squash all the rumours.'

'Rumours?'

Tahlia bit her lip, breathing slowly, willing her blood to cool and her heart to slow. 'There have been a lot of rumours about the company lately,' she said more carefully. Had she messed up? 'You know, about how much financial trouble they're in.'

'Oh?'

She shrugged. 'I'm surprised that a man as smart and as finger-on-the-pulse as you would want to get on board with a company obviously in trouble. There's even a lawsuit going because Raquel messed up.'

'That's been settled.'

Tahlia frowned. 'How do you know?'

'I…' Darrington rubbed his jaw '…heard it on the grapevine.'

'Okay,' she said slowly. 'And why did you come here?'

He leant back in his chair. 'I like a challenge.'

'You're not worried?'

He shook his head and stood up. 'No. Are you?' He moved around the desk and leant on the edge, looking down at her, his arms crossed. 'Why would you stay on if the company is in trouble?'

Tahlia looked up at her boss, appreciating his move to that of dominance, and his wide shoulders. He was looking down at her with his dreamy blue eyes, his profile all power and his lips so enticing... It was a good move, to show who was boss.

'I've got friends here,' she said evenly. 'They need their jobs and I figure I'm helping by staying, you know.' She shrugged and stood up. Had she been too honest? 'I've put a lot of work into this place; it would be hard to walk away.' Incredibly hard, but if she had to go she was determined on doing her bit first.

She was close, just having the height advantage due to the fact he was leaning his cute butt on the edge of his desk and she was wearing heels.

She took a step closer, her brain stumbling for what she could do to soften the guy up. 'So I'm here and eager to do whatever I can to get the company back on track, on plan, on the path to success and happiness for all.'

Case stood up. 'Well, we'll do our bit as best we can then, yes?'

Tahlia looked up into his face, fixing her gaze on his sapphire-blue eyes that were looking down at her, slightly narrowed as though trying to make her out. 'Sure, but there's one thing I have to know first,' she said.

'Yes, what's that?' he asked, his gaze dropping to her mouth.

Her mind went blank.

He was so close.

Her heart thundered in her chest. She moved, stumbled, reached out and touched his smooth silk tie and his hard chest underneath, looking up.

Their lips met.

His mouth quivered beneath hers, softened, yielded, and danced with hers.

He tasted as sweet and spicy as he smelt, like cinnamon toast and coffee…and his lips weren't firm, they were soft, hot and intoxicating.

Heat rushed through her body and the urge to deepen the kiss, wrap her arms around his body and drown in the man almost swamped her.

Tahlia pulled back, letting the silk slide through her fingers. 'O-kay,' she breathed. 'Thank you.'

His eyes glittered. 'What was that?' he croaked, his voice husky.

'I'm…I'm pretty sure it was a…kiss,' she offered softly, staring at his mouth, her own tingling with a need for more. The crazy desire to push up against his body and try that again throbbed deep inside her.

'Yes.' He straightened his tie and tightened the knot, smoothing the silk flat against his shirt. 'Why?'

Her mind clambered for an answer. She had no idea how it had happened. Who had kissed whom? Oh, gawd. How had that happened?

'Just checking,' she said as casually as she could, swinging around and striding to the door on legs that felt spongy. She had to save this embarrassing situation and turn it around to her advantage.

'Checking what, may I ask?'

OFFICIAL OPINION POLL

ANSWER 3 QUESTIONS AND WE'LL SEND YOU
4 FREE BOOKS AND A FREE GIFT!

0074823 ||||||||||||||||||||||||||||||||| FREE GIFT CLAIM # 3953

YOUR OPINION COUNTS!

Please tick TRUE or FALSE below to express your opinion about the following statements:

Q1 Do you believe in "true love"?

"TRUE LOVE HAPPENS ONLY ONCE IN A LIFETIME."
- ○ TRUE
- ○ FALSE

Q2 Do you think marriage has any value in today's world?

"YOU CAN BE TOTALLY COMMITTED TO SOMEONE WITHOUT BEING MARRIED."
- ○ TRUE
- ○ FALSE

Q3 What kind of books do you enjoy?

"A GREAT NOVEL MUST HAVE A HAPPY ENDING."
- ○ TRUE
- ○ FALSE

YES, I have scratched the area below.

Please send me the 4 **FREE BOOKS** and **FREE GIFT** for which I qualify. I understand I am under no obligation to purchase any books, as explained on the back of this card.

4 FREE BOOKS AND A FREE GIFT

N5KI

Mrs/Miss/Ms/Mr _____ Initials _____

BLOCK CAPITALS PLEASE

Surname _____

Address _____

_____

Postcode _____

THE READER SERVICE™
FREE BOOK OFFER
FREEPOST CN81
CROYDON
CR9 3WZ

NO STAMP
NECESSARY
IF POSTED IN
THE U.K. OR N.I.

Her mind spun. What? How he kissed? That he was willing? That she could rise to any challenge for the job? That she was a babbling klutz around the man? She touched her tingling lips. *That he liked her?*

She couldn't help but smile. 'That *you* sent the flowers.'

TO: *KeelyR@WWWDesigns.com*
CC: *EmmaR@WWWDesigns.com*
FROM: *TahliaM@WWWDesigns.com*
RE: Men

Rub your good luck in, why don't you? And I'm not protesting, I'm explaining. A girl's gotta do what she's gotta do.
Tahlia

CHAPTER ELEVEN

***Sagittarians—watch out,
you may get more than you bargained for.***

CASE sagged on to the edge of the desk, gripping the edge of the timber tightly. What in hell—or heaven—was she doing to him?

He rubbed his jaw. Reading his mind? Doing what he'd decided wasn't a good idea? Taking the plunge and finding out if the feeling was mutual?

Hell, yes.

He had no idea how that had happened… Had he kissed her? Hell, he'd wanted to. He may have leant that bit closer, made it happen.

What a kiss!

She was more than a breath of fresh air—she was a spring breeze, warm and sensuous, encouraging a clean break from the past, the promise of something new and exciting.

He stared at his office door, his heart still pumping hard, his blood hot, his whole body still in reaction to those sweet soft lips that had teased him with a hunger that he longed to sate, slowly and sensually through the night with her.

And what a night it would be…exploring the magic that sparked between them like electricity, short-circuiting sense and setting off fires.

Case stood up, raking his hands through his hair. Dammit. This wasn't the time.

He tried to laugh. That kiss had been one hell of a surprise. And he'd brought it on himself. He should have learnt by now that rash actions, like sending those flowers, led to trouble. Beautiful, radiant, curvaceous and irresistible trouble. A woman who he shouldn't be engaging until after the staff assessments were done.

A relationship was built on honesty and how could he be honest when he was pretending he wasn't himself?

Sure, she saw him as an almost-equal, saw him as he was…him. Hell, she would probably be perfectly suited to take over this position herself once he was done here.

He loved the way she talked to him—no airs, not a grace in sight and enough blunt barbs to sink a ship.

Would she be the same if she knew who he was? That he owned this company and several more? That he was so much more than the executive-on-the-way-up that he pretended to be? Would it matter to her?

It had mattered to Celia. She'd totally conned him into believing she loved him. That she couldn't get enough of him, that she'd die if she wasn't his for ever.

He'd never had anyone feel like that about him before, had been convinced it couldn't happen if he didn't have that same intensity and commitment. Had married her anyway and had done all he could to live up to her adoration.

He had been such a fool.

The fax machine bleated. Case ignored it. He knew who it was from, same time every day.

He hadn't had a clue with Celia. Not when the 'simple' wedding to seal their love had turned into a three hundred guests media extravaganza because it was her 'special' day. Not when the Melbourne penthouse hadn't been big enough and a twelve-room mansion on the park was what she wanted, because they did want to start a family. And not when her desire to see the world didn't include him, because he had to stay at home and work for their future.

He had been an idiot. He'd rushed into Celia because she hadn't wanted him to think straight. He wasn't about to make the same mistake again.

This time he was older, wiser and in control.

Case moved to the fax machine, plucked the paper from the tray and went back to his desk, sitting down in his large leather chair, running his tongue across lips that begged for more.

Was the ball in his court? Did he want to return it? Hell, yes. No matter what had happened with Celia, there was no way he was going to miss out on discovering what lay beneath Tahlia Moran's captivating layers—in due course, after his work was done.

He laid out the fax in front of him, forwarded from his head office. Since his mother had discovered the fax machine she'd committed herself to keeping him informed of the entire Darrington family tree via the fax.

She knew he was hard to catch, always on the go, busy-as-hell with his businesses and she'd given up on trying to talk to him 'like normal people' did on the phone and had found an alternative.

It was endearingly crazy. It wasn't as if he needed

to know what operation his father's sister's mother-in-law was having, who his cousin was dating or what the cook served for dinner last night, but he had to love her.

The curse of the only child, he guessed. Who else was she going to tell? His father was always busy— too busy for much except eating and sleeping and, of course, work.

His mother was still waiting for him to retire, so that they could have some time together, and his father could live life...only business came first.

Case jerked to his feet and strode to the door. He'd made enough mistakes where work was concerned. He wasn't going to wait until business fell into place to live... And at this moment living meant Tahlia...and discovering everything about her.

Case couldn't wait.

He gripped the door handle and paused. He'd have to be careful. He'd romance her in a leisurely way, with deliberate style and elegance, ensuring this staff assessment was done before he let himself drown in those sea-green eyes and luscious lips.

He wasn't going to mix business with pleasure.

Tahlia couldn't stop smiling.

Oh my God, she'd kissed her boss! And he'd been incredible.

She'd never considered an office romance before— old, crusty executives not being her thing—but right at this moment an office romance didn't seem such a bad idea.

She bit her lip. The guy could kiss and was more

than easy on the eyes and made her feel things in places she hadn't known existed.

Darn it, but this was all wrong.

She was here for a reason and she hadn't ever failed to complete a goal.

Darrington seemed to know nothing about doing the Marketing Executive job and had even less interest in finding out how to do it. How could he manage the whole design and sales team if he didn't want to know what they were doing?

She sighed. He could be a nice guy but the fact remained that she had to do right by the company.

She punched Raquel's extension. It was almost a shame to have to 'out' his failings to Raquel. Maybe Raquel wouldn't have a total hissy-fit when she found out she'd hired a guy who couldn't do the job and seemed more interested in the staff than doing what he was hired for.

Maybe she wouldn't fire him but demote him. She could put him on as Tahlia's assistant, or somewhere in Personnel…he seemed to be interested in people.

'Wilson.'

'It's Mr Darrington's assistant here,' she said in a meek soft voice. 'Would he be able to schedule a meeting with you at, say…eleven on Thursday?' Tahlia held her breath. The week should be enough to gather the evidence that would support her case, if the Rottie agreed to the timing.

Raquel was notorious for messing people around just to make sure they knew the hierarchy—she was the boss and could do what she wanted. Tahlia would probably have to beg and grovel to get an appointment with her any time this month.

'Mr Darrington. Yes. Of course. Not a problem.' And she rang off.

Tahlia put the phone down in the cradle, staring at it, her stomach leaden. What was that? Raquel never just accepted a time without argument. Something was up...

'Hey,' a familiar deep voice said.

Tahlia's skin rippled as though a thousand butterflies had brushed her body. She looked up at Case. 'Hey.'

'I need to talk to you.'

She stood up, trying to suppress a smile. Couldn't he get enough of her? She sobered. What could possibly have Raquel bowing to him? His good looks, his playboy eyes or that smile?

She narrowed her gaze, running her eyes over the man again, from the tip of his shiny black shoes to the tip of his spiky haircut. It didn't matter.

By the end of the week she'd know every inch of this guy, inside and out. She'd discover all his secrets.

Tahlia's gaze moved to Case's mouth. She probably should avoid those lips. 'What can I do for you, Mr Darrington...Case?' she lilted.

He paused.

She watched his brow furrow. Oh, gawd. Had she got her signals crossed? Had the flowers been from someone else entirely? Had her clever saving-face parting proved she was crazy and she'd just made the biggest fool of herself for no reason at all or had she just scared him off with that incredibly stupid and impulsive kiss that had come out of nowhere?

She tipped her head. He didn't seem like the sort of guy who would scare easily.

He moved closer. 'I don't mean that I'm not flattered or that I didn't enjoy—'

Heat rushed to her cheeks. Oh, gawd. How could she have been so stupid? 'So you didn't send the flowers?'

'I did, actually.'

She tapped the pen on her chin. She had known it! He *was* interested in her, at least enough to send her flowers on Friday—and by goodness that kiss had said as much. He hadn't been exactly bone-cold beneath her lips—far from it.

He was putty in her hands.

She stared at his mouth again. It would just be so easy to lean forward, take a step, tiptoe and kiss him once more, wrap her arms around that firm, hard body.

She froze. To soften the guy up for an interrogation of his motives, not for anything else.

Her whole body ached. 'Then?' she blurted. 'What? It was a mistake? The flowers were sent to the wrong address and it wasn't me you were thinking of? It was someone else entirely and I took it to mean that you were as interested as your amazing blue eyes said you were and—'

Case stepped forward, the distance between them gone. He lifted his hand and touched her lips with his finger, stilling the words rushing from her mouth. 'The kiss *was* amazing.'

The echo of her embarrassing jabbering faded in the wake of the look that shone in his sapphire-blue eyes, the incredible intimacy in his touch, the flames that scorched through every nerve in her body.

She couldn't look away and couldn't move.

He drew his finger back, watching her mouth, the tip of his finger brushing her bottom lip sending bolts of desire through her.

'So?' she whispered.

He dragged in a deep slow breath. 'I…I don't think it's appropriate for me to—'

She stood taller. 'Of course.' Tahlia nodded tightly, trying to fight the surge of heat in her veins.

She would never have considered crossing the line herself under normal circumstances. How could she have thought a man like Case would cross it just because of her?

Had she really thought he'd be some office playboy looking for a quick roll in the copy paper? That the man could be flattered into blurting out his background and connections so she could use them against him?

She shook her head. 'I understand. I am your personal-assistant-cum-glorified-secretary and I'm sure you don't want any scandals on your CV.'

'It's not that.'

She stiffened. 'It's not? You're not worried about what an affair with your PA could do to your future?'

'An affair?'

She bit her lip. Oh, darn, where had that come from? How could she say so many stupid incriminating things around him? 'Well, I guess I could be thinking along those lines,' she said more carefully. If he wasn't sitting in her chair and messing with her workplace. 'And

I wasn't going to be so forward to suggest anything as threatening as a relationship.'

He crossed his arms over his chest. 'Why would you think I'd be threatened by a relationship?'

She shrugged. 'Most men are.'

He dropped his arms to his sides. 'I'm not most men.'

She swallowed hard. 'I can see that. So, if it's not your employment future you're worried about—'

'No.'

'Then?' She looked towards the ceiling. Please let there not be an unrequited love, a dead girlfriend, an ex with a brood of kids. She caught herself. She didn't care.

He slipped his hands into his pockets. 'I already guaranteed you that I wouldn't get too personal with my assistant.'

Relief washed through her like spring rain. 'I'm sure I could overlook that under the circumstances,' she said softly, smiling. Back to Plan A—flirt him into making a fatal mistake.

'And those circumstances are?'

Tahlia looked at her heels, wishing she didn't feel quite so much for the idea. 'That your assistant is me.'

CHAPTER TWELVE

Too many cooks spoil the…bachelor?

'HELLO, handsome.'

The redhead stepped out from behind a large fern in the hallway, her modest attire doing nothing to dampen the gleam in her eyes.

Case stopped. 'Good afternoon, Chrystal,' he offered casually, looking past her to where he wanted to go.

'Case,' she lilted, fluttering her lashes and looking up into his eyes.

'Is there something I can do for you?' he asked, cringing. He had a fair idea what the woman wanted and there was no way he was going there.

'Actually, yes,' she purred, leaning into him as though she still had her revealing top on. 'I was wondering if you'd like to go out with me some time, you know, like on a date.'

Case swallowed hard. 'I'm flattered by your offer, but I—'

She touched his arm, pouting. 'You want to get to know all your staff, don't you? Well, some of your staff are worth getting to know better.'

Tahlia's smiling eyes leapt to his mind.

Chrystal stroked his arm. 'And there's only so much you can find out about a person by working with them.'

'Ye-es,' he said slowly, the idea tumbling through his mind.

She sighed deeply. 'I understand that it's just so much easier for some people to open up to others after hours, away from the workplace.'

He nodded slowly. 'Look, it's been lovely talking to you but I have to get back to work.'

'Don't you think I'm pretty?'

Case froze. He was on dangerous ground. He knew more than anyone what a woman scorned was capable of. 'Yes, but—'

She reached up and stroked her fingers down his cheek. 'So don't you think you should give "us" a chance?'

Us? Case stepped back. 'I'm sorry, but I can't.' His mind spun. 'I'm just not…up to it.'

The woman's forehead creased. 'Okay, but whatever the problem is, I think I could help.'

He sucked in a deep breath. 'It's something that only time can heal, I'm afraid.'

'Oh?' She touched her palm against his chest.

'Yes,' he rushed on, extricating himself from her hand. 'I'm not ready. I can't. I've just been divorced, only a few months ago…and I can't. It was tough. Nasty. You know, bad.'

Chrystal's eyes widened. 'Oh.'

'So thank you for your kind offer, but—'

'I understand,' she said softly, patting his shoulder. 'Sure. I get it. Just know I'm here for you…for anything, even talking, if you need to.'

He sighed. 'Thanks.' He sidled past her, shaking his head. He couldn't believe he'd said that to her. It *was* the truth. He'd been divorced…nearly twelve months ago. And although he'd dated on and off, he wasn't dating anyone manipulative and self-serving like Celia. No chance in hell.

Case detoured via Sales. She had been right about one thing, though.

He glanced into the Sales Director's office, at Tahlia, bending over her desk, gathering files, juggling coffee and balancing a pen between her lips. Was he asking too much of her?

Doing her job and helping him was a big ask. But by the gleam in her eyes she seemed to be enjoying the challenge.

He was glad she thrived on it. He liked being near her. Had enjoyed the day with her, having her leaning close to him, her perfume sweeping around him, her warm body close, her sweet voice explaining patiently the ins and outs of the place.

He knew enough about WWW and what a Marketing Executive did; now all he wanted was to know about her.

Any time he managed to get her mind off the business at hand she started asking questions he couldn't possibly answer about himself, yet.

She was driving him crazy.

She swung around.

'What are you doing for dinner tonight?' he blurted.

She lifted an eyebrow.

Case moved forward and plucked the pen from her lips, searching her eyes for the answer. 'I'd like to take you to dinner.'

She hesitated.

'Somewhere nice.'

'O-kay. Sure. Why not? We can get to know each other a bit better. You know, you could tell me all about yourself,' she rushed on.

'Yes.' He smiled. 'Ditto.'

'Ditto it is.' She shot him a smile, sweeping out of the door, her eyes glittering.

TO: *TahliaM@WWWDesigns.com*
CC: *EmmaR@WWWDesigns.com*
FROM: *KeelyR@WWWDesigns.com*
RE: Baby shower

Gals,

Re my baby shower on Saturday. No strippers—my mother is coming. (This is not a hen night, that's for Em. Save stud for then. My mum is not coming!) Have you met our born-again virgin, Chrystal? Yes, she's taken a vow of…da-da da-dum…celibacy. Is the world still the right way up? Chrystal is a virgin wearing a skirt that covers not only her thighs but her knees! And has a blouse *covering* her breasts. Who said the impossible isn't possible?

K

'How do you get a good guy?'

Tahlia stared at Chrystal's reflection in the mirror. 'I don't know. I'll let you know when I get one.' Her mind tripped to Case and she shook her head. She wasn't sure he was a good guy and he wasn't hers. 'You should probably ask one of the others.'

'True.' Chrystal nodded slowly, brushing her wild hair back and tying it at her nape, doing a good imitation of a school marm. 'You're as messed up as me, only more socially acceptable.'

Tahlia shot her a look. 'Gee, thanks. Why do you say that?' Did she have a 'Romantically Challenged' label stuck on her forehead?

'You're not caught up in the must-haves.'

She swiped her lips with her Peach Passion lipstick. 'I have a career, an apartment, a car and investments. What else could I possibly need?'

'You're joking, right?' Chrystal's eyes widened. 'Even I've worked out that it's not about material things. It's about the people in your life. And sure, I know, I've had a lot of people in my life, men mostly, but it's about keeping them there, you know, people that care for you.'

Tahlia stared blankly at the woman she'd known had hidden depths, but had never realised just how deep.

Chrystal sighed heavily. 'And you need a good man to give you a good—'

'I don't think so. I've done very well without a man in my life, and I don't intend to get one until I get my career all sorted out,' she rushed on. Which, if all went to plan, shouldn't be long, right after she sorted out Darrington.

Chrystal shrugged. 'Could be too late. All the good ones will be gone.'

Tahlia felt the words echo down her spine, and down, settling heavy in her toes.

'All I'm saying is, don't leave it too late,' Chrystal said softly, collecting her handbag.

'Is that what this makeover is about? Finding someone to share the rest of your life with before it's too late?'

'Yes,' Chrystal snapped, flicking a stray strand of her hair back. 'And there's nothing wrong with it.'

'Of course not. If that's what you want.'

'And you don't?'

Tahlia moved towards the door. She did not. How could she? Most people went into relationships blindly, not realising the cons. She'd seen the cons close-up and it was not pretty. She didn't want that.

A fling here or there she could do, but that was it.

'I have to go,' Tahlia said softly. 'I'm still at Mr Darrington's office, so send anything or anyone after me there, okay?'

'Absolutely.' Her eyes shone. 'You know all you have to do is ask and I'll be there. I don't know why you're looking after Case Darrington when you could be looking after your own stuff in the comfort of your own office…'

Tahlia interrupted. 'I know, but I have to do this.'

'Like closure for that promotion that you didn't get?'

She paused, holding the handle to the ladies' room. 'Something like that.'

'Well, when you've had enough closure—'

'Absolutely.' She yanked open the door. It wouldn't be long and she'd close the door on her Director of Sales position and be in her rightful one, with Case somewhere far more suitable.

Chrystal sashayed towards her. 'What do you think about mixing business with pleasure?'

Tahlia swung to face Chrystal, her mouth open. Did

she have that 'Lusting after the Boss' label on her fore-head too?

'Don't look so shocked. I know I've dated nearly everyone in the building—'

She was asking for herself? 'In general, not a good practice, but sometimes it's unavoidable.' Like flirting with Case. 'Why?'

Chrystal sighed, clasping her bag to her chest. 'Just this guy I really really like. He's sort of conventional and uptight like you.'

'Thanks.' Tahlia moved through the door.

Chrystal followed. 'Although he did say that he was still getting over the wounds of a really nasty divorce and couldn't entertain a relationship...he's a real wounded soul...and I want to help heal him.'

Tahlia sighed. Poor girl. The last thing she would ever want to get was tied up with a guy with those sort of issues. 'Don't get your hopes up. A guy like that...' Could seriously be a problem. 'Will have so many issues you may not have a chance for happiness.'

'Maybe, but he's so handsome and hot. I think he's worth a try.'

'Good luck.' Tahlia sighed. At least her parents had started out well, without lies, without issues that would destroy what they had. Her father had managed that on his own.

She would never go near a guy like that. Too much to deal with, too hard to wade through the baggage, too much like asking for trouble and disappointment.

Chrystal fluttered her fingers at her. 'Good luck to you, too.'

Tahlia didn't need luck. She had Case to practise her

arts on tonight and a list of criteria for her ideal mate. She had nothing to worry about.

TO: *TahliaM@WWWDesigns.com*
CC: *KeelyR@WWWDesigns.com*
FROM: *EmmaR@WWWDesigns.com*
RE: Baby Shower

Of course all the studs are booked for my hen night. Only the cakes, clown (joking) and cocktails (non-alcoholic) are for your shower. Can't wait. Counting down the days.

Saw Chrystal. Will all her work on herself pay off? Dunno. But Liam can't get enough of Chrystal... he's breaking and losing stuff all over his cubicle so he can put in acquisitions to her. At least twice a day...and she *hasn't* noticed!

I think it's someone else who has caught her eye. But who? Maybe someone from outside work.

Em

CHAPTER THIRTEEN

*Tahlia's rule number 103: when in doubt,
wear black and show a lot of leg.*

TAHLIA threw another dress on to the bed. She had to get exactly the right outfit for tonight—one that said she was cool, calm and collected.

The phone rang.

Tahlia dropped the coat hanger, the outfit dropping to her feet. Please let it not be Case. She didn't want him to cancel…

She snatched up the phone. 'Tahlia, how may I help you?' she chimed.

'Hello, honey, how is everything with you?'

She swallowed hard, the butterflies in her belly subsiding. 'Mum. I didn't expect to hear from you again so soon.'

'Can't a mother ring her daughter to find out if she got the promotion?' There was a pause. 'Surely they've made a decision by now.'

Tahlia dragged in a deep breath. She couldn't do this a moment longer. She couldn't lie again, not even to spare her mother's feelings, or to save herself a lecture on how she should have got it. 'I didn't get it.'

A long pause. 'You're kidding, right?'

'No, Mum. Truly. They got someone else.' And what a someone else he was.

'Oh, honey…' Her mother tsked.

She shrugged. 'I did the best I could. I put in the hours. I did the extra mile but the General Manager just felt some new blood was better for the company at the moment.' And hopefully her moment would still come.

'Of course you did.'

She sat on the only edge of the bed not covered in clothes. 'Don't worry, I'll keep working for it.'

'Tahlia, honey. I know I've pushed you to make something of yourself but you can't just focus on work; you need a life too.'

She froze. 'What?' This couldn't be her mother.

'You can't leave it too late,' her mother warned. 'You're not getting any younger.'

'Mum,' Tahlia gasped. She didn't want to hear this. She'd done everything to live up to her mother's aspirations for her; she couldn't change the rules on her now. 'What's going on?'

Her mother sighed heavily. 'I know I haven't exactly been a great example to you with men. What with your father—' Her voice got tighter. 'Then with ignoring the whole species. But I figured I'd already had love, my time, my lessons—'

'So, *now* you want me to find a man?' Her voice broke into a high-pitched squeal.

'Honey, I want you to be happy.'

She shook herself. 'I'll be happy when you're proud of me.'

'Oh, baby. Of course I'm proud of you. I've been proud of you since the moment I saw you.' Her mother's voice thickened.

Tahlia nodded tightly, her chest warm.

'You know that, right? But look…I didn't call about your promotion… I went out at the weekend…with a friend of mine…'

'What is it, Mum?' Her mother didn't usually beat about the bush.

'And I'd like you to come around next week for dinner,' her mother asked tentatively.

'Why? What's going on?' she blurted. She hadn't had a meal with her mother since…for ever. She was always too busy.

Her mother sighed. 'I want you to meet someone.'

Tahlia swallowed hard. 'Your friend? You've met someone?' Her blood ran to her toes. How could her mother do it? How could she let herself take another risk? When the last one had cost her so very much.

'Yes, he's been asking me for ages and I finally just went out with him and it was…so nice. Will you come and meet him, honey? It would mean a lot to me.'

'Of course I will,' she said in a rush and she rang off, placing a hand on her chest.

What in heaven's name could induce her mother to want a man in her life again? How could she trust one? It was just not possible.

Was it?

Case was losing it. He had to be. He had meant to take the romancing of Tahlia Moran slow and steady, not ask her to dinner.

It had been a spur of the moment thing, and he had to admit that it felt great. For the first time in a year he wasn't beating himself up about Celia. His mind was totally absorbed elsewhere.

It was crazy how one woman could haunt him while another one pushed so many buttons he felt as if he was going to short-circuit if he didn't drag her to him and taste her lips.

His blood stirred at the thought…

He sobered. No. He'd pushed those thoughts down to work with her today and it had worked. He'd survived her perfume, her soft looks, sweet voice and that long fringe that begged to be brushed back so he could see her emerald-green eyes.

Hell. It was bad enough at work. What had possessed him to further the torture? He couldn't trust himself around her, let alone out at night.

He'd wanted a challenge…

He rapped on Tahlia's door. The building was well located on a good side of town, with great street appeal. It wasn't too old, but old enough to have established gardens and that lived-in homeliness about it. All in all, a good investment. She'd do well with it, despite it being on the first floor and liable to be lacking the requisite view of the city for optimal capital gains.

Case reached for his tie. Not there. He was going casual…and the fact that he truly liked this woman was terrifying. The other women he'd dated over the last six months were all predictable, uncomplicated and easy to be with because they were no threat to him.

He couldn't say the same about Tahlia.

He'd survive tonight, take it slow. It wasn't a hot, brief, passionate affair he was after but something more serious, something he wanted to think about, something to take time over…something that was going to last. That couldn't happen until he could tell her all she wanted to know, and more.

He wanted to tell her how he had started his first business at twelve, how he had invested money in the stock market at eighteen, how hard he had worked in college to buy into his first business.

He straightened the collar on his mauve shirt, tucking it in tightly against his black trousers and adjusting the fit of his black jacket. For now, he'd have to play this cool.

The door opened.

Tahlia stood like a vision in the doorway. Her hair was in another spiky knot at the back of her head, but her make-up was darker, richer, highlighting the colour of her eyes, the silky creaminess of her skin and the deep red lips that beckoned him.

A black dress clung to every luscious curve of her body, plunging low over her breasts, delighting his mind and hands with their gentle softness. Thin straps held the slip of fabric on her, straps that looked so easy to slide off her smooth shoulders…

His body ached.

His heart thundered.

His blood fired to her call.

'Case,' she said, her voice sweet and soft. 'You look great… It's great… I'm so glad you came…' She paused. 'I'm happy to see you.'

He couldn't help but smile. She looked so together… The staff at WWW Designs had only praise for the woman and her competence. Did he make her nervous? 'You thought I wouldn't come?' he asked carefully,

trying to slow his heart and regain control. 'How could
I stand *you* up?'

'The thought crossed my mind…like the flowers.
That tonight was an impulse that you weren't going to
follow through on.' She gave a soft shrug. 'I don't want
you to be here if you don't want to be here.'

He straightened tall. Dammit. He'd never failed to
follow through on anything in his life; he damned in
hell didn't want to give her the wrong impression. 'I
assure you there's no other place I'd rather be but with
you tonight.'

She smiled, her cheeks flushing softly. 'Shall we
go?'

'You're not going to invite me in…to meet your
fish?' Case cast a glance behind her, up a polished
timber hallway to where he could just see a cream sofa.
He could tell a lot from a person's home and he wanted
to know everything about this bewitching enigma.

'*Would* you like to come in?' she offered carefully,
glancing up at him with her sea-green eyes and a coy
smile on full red lips that he couldn't afford to taste
again, just yet.

His body ached, impatient for more of her. He swung
his attention to the landing. 'No. That's okay.
Reservations and all. Maybe later.' He cringed. That
sounded as if he wanted to—do all the things to her
that had been running through his mind all day.

'Maybe,' she said softly, her mouth twitching as she
pulled the door closed.

Was she playing with him? Teasing him? She sure
as hell was hitting the mark. He wanted to pull her into

his arms, smother those red lips with his mouth and strip off the layers that she wore.

'Case,' she whispered.

He pulled his gaze from her sweet mouth. 'Yes?'

'Dinner?'

'Yes.' He urged his feet to move, despite every inch of him wanting to stay, somewhere quiet, somewhere where he could explore Tahlia Moran, Director of Sales, with the utmost care and attention.

He followed her to the lift, watching her hips, her shape, her body move in that incredible dress, an incredible amount of smooth leg flashing with every step.

A split ran up the right side of the dress to her thigh, affording him far more than he could cope with seeing of her very nicely shaped, very smooth-looking leg.

Blood rushed southward, hot and fiery. His hands itched to swing the woman into his arms and show her just what sort of danger she was toying with.

He clenched his fists by his sides, breathing deep and slow, pulling his gaze from her mesmerising sway and tantalising show of flesh, watching the floor in front of him.

So much for staying in control…

Tahlia waited in Case's silver Saab for him to come around to her. She needed the space to catch her breath. She wasn't sure who she was kidding, who was playing who— The man was driving her wild.

The way he looked at her set her ablaze, his deep voice echoing through every nerve, his touch…almost too much to bear.

How could he be so calm?

Yes, the man had reacted to her dress. Thank God. It had taken her long enough to pick it out. Tonight had to be just right to gather the info she required to highlight Raquel's mistake.

Her heart had leapt up her throat at Case's suggestion that she invite him in. She had been sorely tempted, her mind throwing up some crazy idea of getting him out of her system.

She accepted that exploring what Case *Tantalising* Darrington had to offer wouldn't just be educational, recreational and inspirational; it would prove that he was an office playboy and deserved the consequences of stealing her promotion with his good looks and connections.

Tahlia touched her lips, closing her eyes and imagining what sort of havoc the rest of Case would have on her body when his kiss had wrecked havoc on her senses.

It was probably a good thing he hadn't accepted her invitation… A public place was far safer.

Case opened the door, holding out his hand for her to alight, his strong clean-shaven jaw close enough to touch, run her fingers down, trail her lips over.

Tahlia took a sharp breath, more than keen to exit from the enclosed space that was filled with the scent of new leather, hot male and his sexy cologne.

She'd think more clearly in fresh air.

His fingers folded around her hand, sealing her palm against his in a connection that felt so good—too good.

Her hand burned where it met his, making her nerves buzz, the cascade of electricity flowing upwards and then sinking deep into her belly. 'Thank you.'

Case drew her close to him, closing her door, looking down into her face with an intensity that sang to her body.

'We're here,' he said suddenly, stepping back.

'Yes.' Tahlia swung to face Bohemia, one of Melbourne's top restaurants. It boasted the best chefs, the best service and the heftiest prices. She wouldn't have expected anything less of the guy. 'Showing off, are we?'

'What do you mean?' he asked, his voice tight.

'I'm sorry. I don't mean to suggest that snob stuff by you bringing me here,' she rushed on. 'Just that your tastes befit a Marketing Executive, that's all.' Even if he didn't know the job and would take far too much time to learn the ropes to help the company now, when it needed help most.

'Oh. Yes. The wage does offer its advantages,' he said casually, catching her hand and drawing her to the entrance.

'I see.' She tried to stir up her resentment again, but failed. She couldn't feel straight with her hand in his— her body was all sensations, all reactions, all tingling for more of Case's attention.

He pushed open the door, letting her hand slip from his other hand as he held it open for her to pass, his gaze going to the slit in her dress. The light in his eyes and the flicker of a muscle in his jaw sent pulses of excitement racing through her.

Tahlia rubbed her palm against her thigh to expel the charge still tingling there. What she could do about the tingling in the rest of her body, she had no idea.

Case weaved through the line of people in the foyer,

beckoning her to follow. 'Reservation for Darrington,' Case said smoothly to the maître d'.

The balding man in a tux smoothed his thin moustache and nodded. 'Your usual table, Mr Darrington?' he asked, sweeping up two menus and swinging around.

'Yes.' Case glanced at her sheepishly. 'That'll be fine. Thank you, Louis.' Case placed his hand in the small of her back, guiding her after Louis.

'So you bring all your women here, do you?' she asked, biting her cheek, fighting an unusual ache around her ribs. 'Not that I mind,' she blurted. 'Or care. I'm sure a man like you must get around and wouldn't be short of offers and it's not like this isn't a nice place to bring dates to show them not only how much you're making but your taste in wine and food, and your style—'

'That's not my intention,' Case offered.

Louis stopped at a small round table which was nestled in the corner of the room. A deep red leather bench-seat curled around the table, against the coffee-coloured wall and a print of a modern artwork with bold strokes and even bolder colours.

A candle flickered under a textured glass shade, the crystal wineglasses gleaming in the light, the wine bottle all too obviously chilling in the ice bucket beside the table, at the ready.

It was one thing to suppose the man was a career Romeo, another thing entirely to see it, feel it, know it. Tahlia glanced back across the busy room towards the door.

Was she just another distraction from doing his job properly?

'You don't like?' he asked, moving closer to her. 'We can go somewhere else if you're not comfortable, if you don't want to stay...'

She lifted her chin, stifling her concerns. This was business, nothing personal. 'Why mess with something that obviously works for you?'

She slipped on to the bench, sliding a little on to the seat in front of the setting on the table, twining her hands together on her lap. 'Nothing wrong with being organised, regulated, into an efficient routine and all that.' Sounded a lot like what she'd do if she was a guy and was dating regularly.

Tahlia glanced up at Case, who was settling himself at the other side of the small table, his knees brushing against hers. 'Doesn't mean this is contrived,' she blurted, blood rushing to her face and southward.

She stared at her place setting and straightened the cutlery. 'That I'm just another woman to pass a meal with and try on for—'

'Hey.' Case reached across the table and held her hand. 'I'm here with you because I want to find out more about you, because I'm interested in who you are, why you're who you are,' he said slowly, his voice deep and his sapphire-blue gaze on hers. 'I'm sorry I didn't make more of an effort with the dinner arrangements but it was short notice and I have a rapport here.'

'That's okay—' she waved her other hand '—you don't have to explain.'

'I want to.' He gave the hand captured in his a gentle

squeeze. 'I don't want you to think for a moment that this isn't special.'

Tahlia frowned. He couldn't mean that. It was just a spiel. He was an expert, after all. A tall, handsome, amazing Casanova. 'Really?' she asked as innocently as she could.

'Yes. I've brought dates here, but no one as inquisitive, observant and amazingly frank as you.'

She couldn't help but smile. 'Sorry. I'm not usually like this.'

'Don't be sorry,' Case said, leaning closer to her. 'I like you just the way you are.'

Tahlia's chest warmed, filling her with a soft heat that radiated outward, making her whole body light and tingly.

She glanced at where his hand covered hers in his warmth, his strength, and she couldn't help but like the feeling, like him.

No, not a good idea. She knew where liking a man got you—into loving a man, trusting a man and depending on him and she wasn't going to experience that sort of vulnerability and loss, ever.

Sure, she respected the way he dealt with the staff but she'd confirmed his total lack of application to the Marketing job and all it entailed.

He had secured her promotion through dubious connections.

'Case…that's an odd name,' she blurted, extracting her hand as slowly and as casually as she could before she did something she'd regret.

'My father's a lawyer,' Case said, drawing his hand back and straightening his setting. 'I think it was my mother's way of tackling his workaholic nature. She's a psychologist. Decided all she had to do to get him to switch on to giving me attention was to say my name. Case wants you. Spend some time on Case.'

'Did it work?'

'Yeah, pretty much.' He shrugged, picking up the bottle of wine from the ice bucket. 'Unless there was a case more important.'

'Case priorities?' she said softly, fighting a smile. She was glad her mother wasn't the only strange one in the world. 'I'm sorry... I do know the feeling.'

'Your dad's into work in a big way?' Case asked, filling her glass.

'Yes. He was.'

'Was? He's retired?'

She glanced around the busy restaurant—the tables all full, the soft murmur of couples doing little to ease the tension that pounded in her chest. 'Deceased.'

'I'm sorry. How did—'

'So am I.' Tahlia gripped her glass. 'Is *your* dad retired?'

'No. Still working, much to my mother's dismay. She's got a list a mile long of all the places she wants to go to, all the things she wants to see, and still he keeps on working.'

'That's sad. Does she have hobbies?' she rushed on, eager to get as far from the issue of her father as quickly as possible.

'Yes. Me.'

Tahlia couldn't help but smile, relief washing through her at his dropping the subject of her father. 'Let me guess... You're her only child and she's trying

to get you married off so you can give her grandchil-
dren, probably contacts you…almost daily…to ensure
her plight is foremost in your mind at all times.'

Case laughed. 'Spot on. How did you know?'

'I'm an only child too.' And she'd been hoping for
years that her mother would start behaving like everyone else's and care about that stuff. Now she was…
Tahlia wasn't so sure she liked it.

'And your mother is after grandkids?'

Tahlia took a sip of the deep bold claret. 'Always
on my back.' He didn't have to know it was all about
work, at least until tonight.

'I guess it's part of the job description. You'll be
just the same when you have kids.'

'No way. I'm going to be nothing like my mother,'
Tahlia bit out. Visions leapt to her of her mother curled
into a shattered ball on the bed she'd shared with her
father, the days of tears, the weeks of silence, the
haunted look in her eyes, still.

'That's what they all say,' Case said lightly, but he
couldn't help but notice the stricken look on her face.
'What? Have I said something…anything to—?'

'Nothing,' she said lightly, picking up the menu.
'Let's order. I'm starving. Chefs in places like these
take for ever in getting food to the table.'

Case nodded, picking up his menu, casting his eyes
over the list of cuisine his restaurant offered. She may
have guessed he brought all his women here, but not
why. And she wouldn't be able to fault the service.
Everyone knew who he was…and no one disappointed
the boss.

He gripped the menu, the words blurring. He was bursting to tell her.

Case took a gulp of the red wine. For the first time since Celia he wanted to tell a woman all about himself, all his assets, all his achievements, including making this struggling enterprise one of the top five restaurants in Melbourne.

He wanted to impress Tahlia, see her awe, hear her praise, see a warmth in those sea-green eyes that was just for him. 'You do want kids, though?'

Tahlia glanced up, her eyes wide. 'Ye-es, at a later stage I would like to have a couple of children,' she said carefully. 'But I wouldn't bring them into a relationship that wasn't absolutely totally stable and loving.'

'Me neither.' He lifted his arm and a waiter arrived at the table at the ready. 'I'd like the quail entrée, Piper's Peppered Steak with the Chef's Best Salad and the Raspberry and Apple Pie with cream.'

The waiter turned to her.

'Quail,' she said, nodding to Case, her eyes bright. 'The chicken breast with garden salad and a chocolate cheesecake.'

'Is your mother local?' he asked, watching her take a sip of the red wine, her lips almost as dark, looking as rich and sweet as cherries, just begging to be tasted.

'Ye-es,' she said slowly, her gaze on him. 'My mother took a job here just after I first moved to Melbourne to work with WWW Designs. I don't blame her for coming too. I wouldn't want to be all alone and she is all alone and I understand that I'm all she has and all—'

Case heard the flood of sweet words from her mouth, saw the shine in her eyes as she dropped her gaze to the setting in front of her, and wanted her. Desperately, totally wanted her...never to be alone.

He swallowed hard. 'God, you're beautiful.'

Tahlia glanced up at him, a soft flush on her cheeks. 'You don't have to resort to flattery to get me to talk,' she said casually. 'Shoe size? Seven and a half. How I take my coffee? Black with no sugar. Where I go on holiday? Anywhere that has a seminar that can help my career. So what do you want to know?'

Case shook his head. 'Can't a guy make an honest comment about his date's extraordinary beauty without it being taken as a means to an end?'

She shook her head. 'No.'

A waiter moved between them brandishing their entrées, the sweet scent of the freshly roasted delicacy wafting around them.

'You seem dedicated to work.' Case stripped the small quail of its meat, the prized morsels melt-in-the-mouth soft. 'Your file is impressive. You've done a lot in a few short years.' He glanced at her, trying to make her out.

She placed her hands in front of her. 'So you finally read my file.'

Finally, for the twentieth time. She was twenty-six years old and had worked diligently, pursuing her career, yet still seemed so young and innocent in so many ways. 'You mustn't have had time for much of a personal life.'

Tahlia put down her fork, staring at him. 'No, not

much of one, but I've had my fair share of boy-friends…if that's what you're asking.'

Case shook his head. 'You are amazingly frank, Miss Moran.'

'You are incredibly nosey, Mr Darrington. Anyone would think you have an ulterior motive.'

'I do.'

'Oh?'

'I'm seriously interested in all my employees, but I don't usually take them out for dinner.'

'And why am I so different?' she asked softly, watching him with narrowed eyes.

'Because you fascinate me.'

She stared at her plate. 'I—'

He'd scared her away. He could see the hesitation in her eyes, hear it in her voice, feel it in every aching muscle in his body.

'Not that I don't usually bend my principles for a pretty woman,' he blurted. 'Or go after something I want…' Dammit, he was digging himself deeper.

She glanced up at him, a soft gleam in her eyes and a knowing smile just touching her lips. 'I know.'

Case leant back in his seat, watching her. Whatever she thought she knew, it made her happier and more relaxed. Who was he to argue?

Whatever she was thinking had put a smile on her face that glowed with a vibrancy that tantalised him.

It couldn't be bad.

CHAPTER FOURTEEN

Emma's rule number two: make love, not war.

TAHLIA chewed on her bottom lip, walking slowly to her front door, every footfall thundering through a body too alert, too aware of Case so close behind her, the warmth of his suit jacket around her shoulders smothering her with his spicy cologne mixed all too enticingly with pure male scent.

Their third date, in as many days, had been wonderful, the food almost as incredible as the company.

It wasn't that she *wanted* to date him, but she found that at work she was so busy with finding files for Case, setting up interviews and doing her own job that she hardly had time to do anything more than admire his dedication to the employees. And he did keep asking her out so she had the opportunity to find out more about him.

Who was she to decline?

At least the plan was working. She was getting to know Case, although she was discovering more about his pets, his parents, his hobbies and his childhood than the details of his career.

Now he was being incredibly tortuous by doing the chivalrous escort-the-girl-to-the-door thing that drove her mind mad with the should-she or shouldn't-she invitations for coffee, inclinations to kiss him, and intense desire to do more than show him the door after the coffee and kiss.

'Thank you for another wonderful evening,' she offered tightly, opening her bag and scrabbling for her keys, pushing the silly notions from her mind.

He was a professional and her boss. Much as she wanted him to be the office playboy, after spending the last few days with him she had serious doubts. He was simply wonderful.

'My pleasure, Tahlia,' he said, her name a mere whisper on his breath.

She shivered, plucked out her keys and fought the jumble for the right one. 'It was great. The mousse was so rich and sweet and smooth—' She glanced up at him—like his voice, like his jaw, like his lips…

'It was,' he said, inching even closer. 'Can I help?'

She watched as he took the keys from her hand and poked the one she'd labelled 'front' in the lock and turned, pushing the door wide.

'Thanks.' Tahlia swept his jacket off her shoulders, the moment when he'd wrapped her in it scored in her memory, his body heat still lingering around her, her heart hammering against her ribs.

She tried to keep that comment he'd made that first night she'd gone out with him, that she was just another date, foremost in her mind, but the rest of the week pressed in on her, smothering her senses with a kindness and a warmth a shallow Romeo just shouldn't have.

She wanted to tell him everything, stay close to him, talk to him all night…and more.

Was this what her mother was feeling? Was this crazy feeling the reason she'd risk so much on a man?

Tahlia looked up into Case's sapphire-blue eyes. 'I lied, you know,' she said softly.

'Oh, yes?' he said, lifting an eyebrow and taking a step back. 'About what, exactly?'

'I haven't exactly had my share of boyfriends.' Tahlia bit her lip. 'No serious boyfriends at all, really.'

'Oh.'

Her belly tightened. 'But don't get me wrong. I have had boyfriends. Plenty. Just no one special, you know, someone who made me feel like—' She caught herself. 'What about you?'

He shook his head. 'No serious boyfriends either,' he said softly, a smile teasing the corners of his mouth. 'But I did… I was…in a serious relationship.'

'And—?'

'And it didn't end well,' he murmured, moving closer. 'But I believe in second chances. Do you?'

She hadn't thought she ever could after what her father did… Hadn't believed she could ever trust a man again, but this feeling, and Case, was special.

She looked up to hand him his jacket, catching his blue gaze and holding it, the gleam residing there fixing her to the spot. 'Yes,' she whispered.

Case lifted a hand to her face, brushing her cheek with his knuckles, pushing back her long fringe, hooking his fingers around her neck and drawing her closer.

His gaze dropped to her mouth.

'Case—' she croaked, moistening her lips instinctively, her whole body aching for him. 'This may not be a good idea—' There was still so much to say before anything happened between them.

He leant down, brushing his lips over hers.

Oh, gawd—yes. Sensation sizzled along her lips, cascading down her body, nestling deep in the pit of her stomach where a yearning ache flared.

He tasted her mouth, teased her lips with his own, drawing up his other hand to cup her face.

Oh, hell, yes.

Tahlia pressed her hands against his hard solid chest, his heart thumping beneath her touch, his warm skin beneath just one thin layer of cotton, all that hard muscle and flesh so close...

He drew back, tasting her lips again. 'You're probably right. Not a good idea...' He brushed her lips with his mouth. 'Not a good idea at all.'

She backed into her doorway, her hands clenched tightly in his shirt. 'Colleagues and all.'

Case followed, his gaze on her lips, his hands on her shoulders. 'Absolutely. Not a good practice.'

'Practise is good,' she whispered, flicking open his shirt buttons and sliding her hands against his warm skin, revelling in the heat of him, the hardness of him, the incredible smoothness.

He sucked in a deep breath, pushed the door closed with his foot and kissed her soundly.

Case's lips caressed hers, soft and sensual. He drew her closer still, running a hand down over her waist, down her hip, down her thigh and up again, moulding her against him.

Oh, by all she'd denied too long, yes.

She popped the rest of his buttons, running her hands

up his hard chest and over his wide shoulders, pushing the shirt from his body.

Case lightened the kiss, as though the cool air of the room had subdued his desire. He dragged in a deep breath.

'We're professionals,' he murmured, trailing kisses along her cheek, over her ear and down her neck. 'We should look at the bigger picture. Not make rash decisions…'

Tahlia pressed her lips against his shoulder, his skin sweet and salty. 'What are the cons?' she whispered. 'Career suicide?'

'No.' Case slipped his hand behind her back, his breath exciting the pulse in her neck. 'Office gossip.'

'Hierarchy complications?' Tahlia suggested, trailing her fingers down the bare flesh of his back and up again. 'Impartiality issues?'

'Not being able to keep my hands off you at work,' Case murmured in her ear, coaxing the zip down at her back. 'In the lift, in the office, on my desk.'

Fire erupted deep inside her. She twined her fingers in his hair. 'What are the pros?'

Case brushed her shoulders with his large hands, sweeping off the straps, letting the dress fall to the floor. His eyes glittered, his gaze travelling up her long legs, over black lace panties to her matching lace bra. 'You.'

She couldn't help but smile, pushing everything from her mind except this moment, with him. It didn't matter who he was, what he really wanted, as long as he wanted her.

She took a step towards him, reaching up and touching his cheek, running her palm down his jaw. 'And this,' she whispered, brushing his lips with hers on tip-toe.

Case swept her into his arms, crushing her mouth.

Tahlia opened herself to him, welcoming the hunger, the heat of his kiss that was only matched by the flames of lust leaping up inside her.

He lifted her into his arms.

She pushed open the bedroom door behind him.

He strode into the room, placing her on to the bed reverentially, drinking in the sight of her. 'Oh, God, Tahlia,' he groaned, tracing her curves with his eyes, his hands following. 'I'm lost. You drive me wild.'

Tahlia ran her hands down his chest, hooking his belt and unclasping it, drawing it slowly from his trousers. 'And crazy?'

'And crazy,' Case whispered hoarsely, unclipping her bra and peeling it from her full breasts.

'I want you too,' she said softly, drawing him down and claiming his mouth. And she did. She burned for him. Wanted him so much she could hardly breathe.

'And practise makes perfect,' she whispered.

Tahlia watched Case sleep in the soft light from the streetlights outside. Wow. She couldn't believe this—how nice he was, how amazingly lucky she was to wake up next to him.

She trailed her fingers down his chest, wondrous at the ripples of muscle, the light scatter of chest hair, the perfection of him.

He caught her hand. 'Hey, that tickles.'

'Sorry, did I wake you?'

'Yes, but it was the nicest way anyone has ever woken me.'

She couldn't help but smile. Gawd, she felt amazing... He'd given so much, shared with her so much. She wanted more, so much more, craved to be closer, know *everything* about Case Darrington. 'Last night was—'

'I know,' he said, his voice deep.

'No regrets?' she whispered.

'How could I have regrets?' Case leant up on his elbow, looking down at her. 'Not a chance.'

'So, can I ask you something?' she asked tentatively, tracing his jaw with the tip of her finger. 'About your last serious relationship—you mentioned it last night.' She needed to know how long ago it had been, that she wasn't a rebound girl to patch some wounded ego.

Case cupped her face. 'It wasn't just a serious relationship... I was married.'

Tahlia froze. Oh, gawd.

'It's okay. I'm divorced—' He frowned. 'I'm not defective... Okay, maybe I am, but I can promise you I won't make the same mistakes again.'

'Should I ask what they were?' she whispered softly, drawing her hand back and placing it on her chest over her heart.

'I wasn't blameless,' Case forced out. He needed to face it, needed to say it. He'd spent far too long blaming Celia for the whole disaster. It was time he accepted his part in it. Needed to, so he could move on and embrace a future with Tahlia.

'I was away a lot, working my butt off to reach my

dreams, my goals, and I lost sight of the fact that Celia had dreams and goals too.'

'Celia was your wife?'

Case swallowed hard. 'Yes. Much as I didn't want to be a trophy husband, my neglect and my obsession with work made her feel like a trophy wife. I regret the pain I put her through. I regret that I turned into my father.'

'And?' she said softly, looking up at him with wide eyes. 'Are you still your father?'

'No, thank God.' He pushed her long fringe back from her face. 'I learnt.'

'Too late,' she whispered softly.

'Yes. While I worked like a maniac she filled her life with things, jewellery and men. By the time I realised what I'd done it was too late; nothing I tried could fix it.'

'Did you love her?'

Case ran his hand down her cheek. 'I thought I did. It was a kind of love, but nothing like—' His voice broke. Like what he was feeling for the woman in his arms.

'I'm sorry.'

'I was too, for a long time, but not now.' He shook his head, drinking in Tahlia's creamy smooth skin. It was time to come clean. He couldn't keep anything from her now. 'Tahlia, I—'

She touched his mouth with her fingers. 'Enough talking.' She drew him down to her, taking his lips with her own, smothering the memory of Celia with the magic of her kiss.

It could wait. They had plenty of time. It was probably something he shouldn't just blurt out anyway. It was something to prepare her for.

At least now he knew for sure. His heart wasn't broken. It was finally alive with the magic of love. He'd found exactly what he had been looking for. Tahlia.

CHAPTER FIFTEEN

***Keely's rule number seven: face your fears
and seize the moment.***

TO: *TahliaM@WWWDesigns.com*
CC: *KeelyR@WWWDesigns.com*
FROM: *EmmaR@WWWDesigns.com*
RE: Chrystal and that look on your face
First, tell all. You haven't looked like this since…
ever. What's up? Are you in love? Has it got some-
thing to do with that man in your chair who fits your
original criteria or have you found a tattoo-wearing,
glass-munching man to turn you on?
And Chrystal is floating around extolling advice
about wounded men like a Florence Night-in-love.
Has Cupid hit?
Em

IT WAS ALL Tahlia could do to sit outside Case's office
and not go inside and taste the magic of his lips again
and again and again.

He was like a drug and she couldn't get enough of
him. Last night had been magical in so many ways and
she couldn't believe she'd been so stupid to deny herself this.

Thank heavens that Case had come along and
opened her eyes to life, to sharing, to him.

Was this what Chrystal was after by chasing every pair of trousers in the building and what her mother had found in the man she wanted her to meet?

TO: *EmmaR@WWWDesigns.com*
CC: *KeelyR@WWWDesigns.com*
FROM: *TahliaM@WWWDesigns.com*
RE: Chrystal and that look on your face.
I'm not saying anything that will later incriminate me, especially where the 'office playboy' is concerned. I will figure out what I'm feeling and in due course share my adventures with my two closest friends.
Definitely *not* shot by arrow-wielding midget.
T

No way was this love. Her mother and father had had something far more sensible than this craziness she was feeling. Besides, she couldn't be in love. She wasn't going to love anyone.

She'd decided when she was twelve that love wasn't for her—about the moment her mother had told her what had happened to her father, that he wasn't ever coming home again.

Love was for suckers, for young, naïve romantics. She was a professional and this was just another necessity to attain her true goal in life—a perfect career, because you could rely on work, you couldn't rely on men.

All men were liars; they didn't share their feelings or their fears and consequently left the world thinking they had jumped, when they could just have befallen a tragic accident.

So Case had shared his failed marriage with her—it didn't mean he was the one that she'd risk everything for... Or was he?

She chewed on her bottom lip. He was divorced... What did that say?

She was never going to subject herself to pain, no matter how amazing Case *Tantric* Darrington was in bed, or how warm his lips were, how safe his arms were or how nice it had been to hear another human being's heartbeat when she had woken up this morning in his embrace.

Chrystal rushed up the hall towards Tahlia. 'Is this a good time?'

Tahlia nodded and waved her closer, anything to distract her from the love issue. So Case was incredibly, wonderfully nice—it didn't mean she liked him. So the guy was great in bed—it didn't mean she wanted him. So she wanted to spend every moment with him—it didn't mean she loved him.

Chrystal sauntered up to the desk, her plaid knee-length skirt doing nothing to hide the exaggerated sway of her hips. 'You won't believe what I just heard.'

Tahlia sat taller and picked up a pen, spinning it in her hand. 'What? Tell me.'

The receptionist leant forward, her blouse not as demure as the D cups she owned beneath it. 'I heard on the grapevine that WWW Designs has just been sold.'

Tahlia gripped the pen tighter. 'Oh, God. No.'

'Yes.'

She dragged in a ragged breath. It couldn't be. It was a mess. Who would want a mess like WWW? The only workplace she'd ever known could be ripped apart, her workmates scattered to all corners of the city, her secure future torn to shreds. 'To whom?'

'Some conglomerate, they say.' Chrystal straightened and examined her nails. 'I'll let you know if I hear what's going on, but someone said it's one of those companies that owns a company that owns another one.'

'But who?' If she knew who was behind it all she'd be able to work out whether they meant to revamp the place and run it, or chop it into little pieces and sell it off to make a nameless profit for a bunch of rich fat-arsed shareholders.

'I don't know, but the guys in Programming said that the first thing these big guys do is bring an expert in and turn the place upside down, weed out the inefficiencies and re-haul, or dissect, depending on the value.'

'I know,' Tahlia said softly, pulling her jacket tighter around her. She hadn't put everything she had into WWW Designs, years of her life, just so that they could sell it off, chop it up and destroy it. *Please, no.*

Chrystal shrugged. 'Nothing to do but give everyone the heads-up so they're all working to top form. Slackers get the sack.' She paused. 'And I'll let you know if I hear anything about the new owners from the rumour mill.'

'Okay. Good, thanks,' Tahlia said, her body numb.

Chrystal swung her attention to Case's door. 'Should *I* tell him?'

Tahlia shook her head. 'I'll do it.' The poor guy was going to be out of his new job if an efficiency expert came in. He'd done nothing except get acquainted with the staff under him, which was all well and good, but if an expert came in they'd want to see him doing the job that he was at least a few weeks off knowing the ins and outs of.

She chewed on her pen. An expert coming in would be perfect to get rid of the Rottie, what with the mistakes she'd made lately, but Case was like a sitting duck.

She stood up. Her promotion would be available again, for sure, if the new owners decided to keep the place running, and poor Case didn't have a clue.

She tossed the pen on to the desk and picked up the file that she'd been making on Case. Some things were more important than her promotion, like doing the right thing for someone she cared about.

Tahlia froze. *Was* she falling in love?

TO: *TahliaM@WWWDesigns.com*
CC: *KeelyR@WWWDesigns.com*
FROM: *EmmaR@WWWDesigns.com*
RE: Chrystal and that look on your face.
Poor Chrystal—if she had her sights on Case she's out of luck. Case is interested in someone else… (Hey, Tahlia—how's it going with lover boy?). After all the work she's done too. Hope she doesn't fall off the virgin-wagon when she finds out… She's so

much nicer like this. Liam certainly thinks so. He's
kicked those nerdy spotty shirts and gone for pastels
and got contacts and a haircut.

Em

Tahlia froze at Case's doorway, looking out through
the full-height windows to the balcony, the existence
of which she usually managed to block out.

The sliding door was open.

Case was out there.

Fear ripped through her like cold steel. 'Case,' she
croaked, her voice closing over.

Case turned. 'Miss Moran. Come to share the glo-
rious morning with me?'

'Yes,' she breathed, dragging her feet like lead
weights across the floor, focusing on the amazing man
who had awakened her to so much. Not the windows,
not the height, not the balcony. 'But inside, okay?'

His brow furrowed. 'What is it?'

'Please.' Tahlia glanced around her, dropping the file
on a chair. It was so high up she could see cars in the
distance that looked like toys ants would play with. 'I
don't like heights.'

Case walked back into the office, sliding the door
closed behind him. 'Do you want to talk about it?'

She shook her head, the memories pressing in on her,
the scream, the silence and the sirens.

He took her hands and directed her to the chair closest to the wall. 'I did notice you didn't have a window
in your office.'

Tahlia nodded, fighting the logic of how many people could guess her fear, and hating herself for it. Her father's face leapt to her mind.

She lifted her chin, meeting his warm gaze. 'It's not something I talk about.'

'Sometimes it helps to share problems.' Case knelt in front of her, holding her hands in his warm ones. 'I'm here for you.'

She couldn't help but smile. How could she not share this with him after he had shared so much with her? 'My father…died.' She sucked in a deep breath. 'He fell from a balcony…there was a loose rail.'

'Oh, God, Tahlia.' Case's voice broke. 'I'm so sorry. I had no idea.'

'Losing my father was tragic for me, for my mum and me, but listening to the whispers was shattering.'

'Whispers?'

'He'd been drinking. He had financial problems. And he was fighting with my mum.'

Case rubbed her hands. 'It *was* an accident.'

'But you wonder… I wonder…if I could have been a better daughter. If I had better marks at school. If I hadn't nagged him to play checkers with me, then he wouldn't have been up there—'

Case swept her into his arms, holding her against his chest. 'Oh, hell, Tahlia.' He stroked her hair back from her face. 'It was an accident,' he said quietly.

'Yes,' she whispered. 'That's what they all said, but—' She had heard the whispers.

'Hey, of course it was an accident. He loved you and your mother very much… He probably just wanted to protect you from his business worries; he didn't want you to think he wasn't the strong, capable man you thought he was.'

She nodded. 'He fell.'

'Yes, and anyone who says he jumped is a fool, who doesn't know how beautiful and loving you are…who doesn't know how much he was loved.'

She nodded. He was right. It wasn't what happened. It was the meaning she placed upon it. She'd spent far too long listening to whispers that didn't matter. She had loved her father and her father had loved them and it had been an accident, a tragic accident that had stolen her father from her.

'Has anyone told you how wonderful you are?' she asked, sucking in a deep breath. Or how easy it could be to fall in love with him?

'Not lately.'

She rested her head on his chest, which held a heart so warm and loving to offer her such understanding and kindness about her father.

Case held her close, staring out of the window, breathing in her sweet scent, feeling her breath slow down, become deeper, her body relax.

He'd never felt so close to another human being than at this moment. Tahlia had finally let another layer slip away. She'd let him in. He'd never known a feeling like this.

It was incredible.

What he'd thought had been love with Celia had obviously just been infatuation, followed by a hefty dose of ego-induced denial. He had never liked admitting mistakes. And marrying Celia had been a whopper.

Working so hard to save their marriage had probably been more for the sake of the marriage than for them— to show himself and his mother that he wasn't his father. He could change.

He had changed. Now he knew what love was. Sure, it was early days, but he knew, deep in his chest, that he couldn't live without Tahlia. She was air to his lungs, reason for his being, the future mother of his children.

It was her.

He should tell her the truth about why he was here, who he was and exactly why he'd lied, before this went further.

'Tahlia,' he murmured softly. Was now the time? She was obviously vulnerable just now.

Hell, to lose her dad in that way... He ached to fix the past, go back and save her father, so she didn't have to deal with it, feel that pain.

She stepped back, sucking in a deep breath. 'Oh, gawd, I totally forgot why I came in,' she said strongly, sounding more like the Tahlia he knew.

'Understandable.'

She shrugged, swiping down her white blouse and short office skirt, taking his attention to her legs, firing his body with memories of the feel of her wrapped around him, of making incredible passionate love to her.

'I need to talk to you.'

He nodded, watching her move to his desk and sit down opposite his chair as though nothing had happened, all cool and collected. She glanced at him and the soft look in her eyes clawed at his gut.

It was time to tell her. There was only one person who knew who he really was and he wasn't about to let Raquel come between them.

There was no reason to wait until after this little assessment was done. Waiting wasn't worth the risk of enjoying anonymity any longer.

Sure, before he would have said he needed assurances before he risked telling her the truth. Assurances that she wasn't another Celia to run knives through his heart. But that wasn't Tahlia.

She was special. Amazing. His.

Case moved to the desk and propped himself on the edge in front of her. It would probably be a good idea to solve her concerns first. 'What is it?' he asked. 'Is there something I can do? Something wrong?'

A shadow flitted across her face. 'Yes.'

Case's gut tightened. He'd do anything to make things right for Tahlia. What else could be wrong?

'WWW Designs has just been sold to some conglomerate,' she said softly, looking up into his face, her eyes wide.

'Oh?' He watched her carefully. Did she know who he was? Please let her not have found out from anyone else.

Tahlia crossed her legs. 'Odds are they'll send an efficiency expert in to assess the way the place is run.'

'They probably will,' he said, breathing out. He'd have to tell her, before this went any further. Better the truth came from him and not from someone else.

'No. I know they will.' She jerked to her feet and paced the floor in front of him. 'Don't you get it? I *know*.'

Case's gut tightened. *'You know?'*

'Yes. I know that Raquel hired you because you knew someone that knew someone and that you're very easy on the eye.'

'I'm easy on the eye, am I?' He couldn't help feeling a thrill when she said it, or the heat that ran through him at the look in her eyes, her sweet voice.

She threw up her hands. 'You are, I assure you, but you're not getting it. It's not about you being a tall, dark, handsome hunk of a guy—'

'Is that all I am to *you*?' he asked slowly, tongue in cheek. He wanted to be so much more than that to her. Was he kidding himself that there was more to this? She had said she wanted an affair... Could he get her to want more?

She stopped in front of him and kissed him on tiptoe. 'No, idiot. Listen, you have to get up to speed and fast. I don't want you to lose your job.'

'Lose my job?' he echoed.

'Yes, you idiot.' She slapped his shoulder. 'You're not exactly the most qualified person for the job, if you hadn't noticed. And sure, you had connections to get you into the position, but with an expert coming in you're going to have to do a lot more than sit in that chair and look at personnel files.'

He pulled her closer, tucking her fringe behind her ear. 'You don't want me to lose my job?'

'No.'

'Why?' he asked, pulling his knuckles back across her smooth cheek to her lips, which were just begging to be kissed.

Tahlia slapped him on his chest, glaring up at him, her heart pounding. 'Because…' Was it too early to say? She knew she felt it—it pumped through her entire body, filling her chest with a warmth to rival the sun. 'Because I think I like you. Okay? Is that what you wanted to hear?'

'Yes. Actually.' He caught her chin in his hand and tipped her face up, wondering whether there was more she wasn't admitting to. 'How can we find out for sure?'

'I can tell you all the things you need to know about the job if you'll let me help you—'

'Tahlia—'

She shook her head, picking up the file she'd made on him and propelling him back to his desk. 'No. You may think you know it all, but truly an expert will wipe the floor with you. You have to know everything.'

Case perched himself on the edge of the desk, holding both her hands. 'Tahlia—'

Tahlia shook her head. 'Just listen. Liam is our top programmer, distracted at the moment by the opposite sex, but the best. He's being poached by our biggest competitor and if thwarted in love will go somewhere else if he doesn't get the right incentives to stay on.'

Case frowned. 'Does Raquel know this?'

'The Rottie? She's so out of touch.'

'The Rottie?' Case echoed, stifling a smile. The woman would certainly be livid if she found out that was what they called her but, he had to admit, it suited her.

Tahlia waved a hand dismissively, slapping the file on to the edge of his desk. 'Keely is heading out on maternity leave in a fortnight and needs to be assured her job will not only be there when she gets back but that she can create website designs at home until she's ready to come back full-time.'

'She could.'

'Emma has accepted an offer from a firm in New York and she's leaving. She brought in *Harold's House* and is marrying the owner of *Harold's House* so it's in WWW's interests to have an open invitation for her to return.'

Case pulled her closer to him, tucking her between his legs, drawing her on to his lap. 'Tahlia, I need to tell you something—'

She smiled. 'I know…' She loved him too. It was crazy but she was going to do this right, unlike her mother. 'Chrystal is a valuable asset but needs far more to occupy her; she's under-motivated and finds herself trouble, a lot.'

'Short frizzy redhead on the prowl?'

'Yes.' Tahlia hooked her arm around his neck, snuggling closer to him. It was time to tell him what she'd been thinking and doing for the last week. 'And me; you need to know something about me. That I was—'

Case smothered her with a kiss that washed away the tension knotted inside her. It was a soft, dreamy kiss, a kiss for a tired soul to melt into.

She finally pulled back, her lips tingling. 'What was that for?'

'To get you to shut up for a minute. I have something important to tell you.'

'Uh-huh.' She sighed, running her tongue over her lips.

Case's gaze dropped to her mouth. He leant closer and brushed his lips over hers again, slowly deepening the kiss, a hand sliding up her waist to cup the fullness of her breast.

She'd never felt so amazing before, so complete, so totally and utterly safe. Nothing could go wrong.

The door burst open.

'What in hell is going on here?' Raquel's nasal whine echoed through the room.

CHAPTER SIXTEEN

The best-laid plans of mice and women.

TAHLIA froze. She broke away from Case and straightened her jacket, casting a look at the Rottie, who looked as if she was about to break some capillaries.

What could she say to save this situation? She had slipped and fallen on her new executive, or just that she was falling in love with him? 'First aid,' she said in a rush, making the space between them larger.

She lurched forward and picked up the file.

Raquel strode into the room. 'Right, Ms Moran. First aid,' she bit out, swinging her gaze to Case, looking as if she was trying to swallow a melon.

Case stood casually where she'd left him, as though being caught by the boss was nothing to him, his eyes still shining and his mouth curved sensuously in her direction, as though all that mattered was her.

Tahlia's chest ached. He was amazing. He had no idea who he was messing with but he was about to find out all about the Rottie's bark.

Would she sack him? Both of them?

She bit her lip. This couldn't happen to Case. He was innocent, a decent guy who'd just happened to get the job she'd been obsessed about.

She had been crazy to care so much about that promotion. Her mum loved her for who she was, was proud of her no matter what she did, was okay with her living her life just the way she wanted to.

She didn't have to be afraid any more—her mother wasn't.

Tahlia moistened her still-tingling lips. She didn't care what happened to her now, but Case couldn't be punished for her stupidity. She loved him.

She touched her chest where her heart echoed her thoughts. She loved him. How it had happened, she had no idea, but she knew there were other jobs but there was only one Case.

She stepped towards the General Manager, who had terrorised the entire office for years, holding the file close to her, her heart thundering in her chest.

She couldn't let Raquel know she'd made a mistake employing Case; she wanted to keep him, no matter what chair he was sitting in.

'It was my fault,' Tahlia blurted. 'Don't blame anyone but me. I was the one who kissed him—he's been nothing but the nicest guy.' She glanced at him. 'Decent and caring and keen to get to know the staff like a good manager of people should—'

'Right,' the Rottie snapped. 'If you'll excuse Mr Darrington and myself, we have business to discuss.'

Tahlia glanced at her watch. Of course that was why the woman was here. It was eleven a.m. and Raquel was right on time.

She should have remembered the Rottie was coming and, dammit, she'd proven Case's weaknesses all too well.

'We do?' Case asked, straightening his tie.

Raquel swung to him. 'Yes. Your assistant arranged for me to come in.'

Case stared at her blankly.

'You didn't know? Where's your assistant? I'll have a few words to say about interrupting my very busy schedule for fictitious meetings. Everyone knows how busy I am keeping this office running smoothly.'

Case swung his attention to Tahlia, the light in his eyes fading. 'Tahlia?'

Raquel stared at Tahlia. 'You? No way. You'd never take a step backward...'

Tahlia's blood chilled. This was not good. 'I need to talk to you,' she offered Case, mentally crossing everything she had that this stopped here.

'*You're* his assistant?' Raquel crossed her arms over her chest. 'I know I said to help the man out, but I never expected you to do *that* much, especially considering...'

'Considering what?' Case asked, his voice deep and cool, his face a mask of stone.

No. This couldn't be happening. She stepped forward, brandishing his file at the man she loved. 'Case—'

Raquel snatched the file from her hands. 'Considering that she's been after the Marketing Executive job for months.'

Case swung to face her. 'Why is Raquel here?'

Tahlia tore her gaze from the incriminating file in the Rottie's hands and fixed her eyes on Case. What could she say?

Would he ever look at her again with those warm blue eyes, whisper sweet words with his deep, smooth voice, touch her lips again with his or hold her in his arms if he knew how crazy mad she had been at him for taking her job?

Raquel flicked through the file and cleared her throat. 'Well, Mr Darrington, I believe I'm here to see just how committed Miss Moran is to her job.'

Tahlia stared at the Rottie, her calm tone sliding down her spine. She wasn't upset? How could she not be barking blue murder at the repeat performance of the last executive, of having a file full of evidence supporting her very questionable decision to employ Case?

'This is fascinating.' She shook the file. 'Documented evidence that you, Mr Darrington, aren't qualified for the position she feels she should have got.' She shook her head slowly. 'And what was that intimacy in aid of? I'd love to hear how you thought *that* could help your cause, unless you've discovered—'

Raquel swung to Case, lifting an eyebrow.

He turned to her, piercing her with a chilling look. 'Tahlia?'

Her name slid from his lips like poison from a broken glass. No. How could he believe that she'd wanted anything other than to be with him after the week they'd spent together, after last night, after they'd shared so much, after she'd surrendered her heart to him?

Tahlia felt the rattle in her chest, staring at the file she'd filled to justify being his assistant, spending time with him, going out with him, wanting to know him.

A tearing ache ripped through her chest as the enormity of what was at stake hit her. She'd been an idiot, making a mess of the one thing that mattered.

She couldn't lose him. She didn't want him fired; she needed him.

'I was stupid.' Tahlia sighed.

Case couldn't be hearing this. There had to be a mistake. There was no way that Tahlia was the sort of woman to manipulate her way up the ladder. Not a chance. Not with all he knew about her, unless it had all been lies.

Could she know who he really was? Had her revelations of all the ins and outs of the employees just been a ruse to ensure she kept his attention when it came to the hirings and the firings?

Raquel swung to face him, tucking the file under her arm. 'Mr Darrington, I'm sorry about this. I take full responsibility,' she said sweetly. 'I just didn't think Miss Moran would go to such lengths to ensure her promotion.'

His gut tightened. Raquel was certainly going to great lengths to ensure *her* position and rightly so; she'd been on shaky ground from the start.

He turned to face the woman he had thought he knew. '*I* was placed in the position *you* were after…so you had to prove there'd been a mistake.' He took the file from Raquel, flicking through the pages, his blood going cold in his veins.

'I was angry. It meant so much to me—' Tahlia blurted, her eyes wide.

Her words hit him full force in the chest. It was true. The only reason she had wanted to be near him was to prove her point.

Celia's face lurched to his mind, her memory a dull

ache to the darkness tearing through his chest. He swung to face the window.

He couldn't have walked right into a relationship with a woman just like his ex-wife, couldn't be attached to a manipulating liar who was just after what he could give her, couldn't have given his heart away to someone who didn't love him for who he was.

He couldn't have done it again.

CHAPTER SEVENTEEN

Tahlia's rule number one: don't fall in love.

TAHLIA crossed her arms in front of her. 'So are you going to fire me?' she asked Raquel, forcing herself to keep her tone soft, really only wanting one answer from the woman with the power—was she going to fire Case and punish him for Tahlia's stupidity?

Raquel smirked.

Tahlia knew the answer. The Rottie wouldn't hesitate to fire *her*. She hated having Tahlia breathing down her neck, spouting ideas on improvement, undermining her authority, especially when Raquel had messed up that contract.

'Fire you?' Raquel snorted. 'Why in heavens would I do that when you're hammering all the nails into your own coffin?'

Tahlia glanced at the Rottie, her mind trying to subdue the storm of emotions to make out what the woman was saying. What was going on?

'That file is interesting reading,' Raquel said, lifting her sculpted nose. 'But I think that little interlude I witnessed takes the cake. Case Darrington isn't a fool.'

'Of course he isn't,' Tahlia said, straightening tall and looking at him by the window, the urge to go to him and hold him, wrap him in her arms and tell him it was all okay burning in her.

Did this mean the Rottie wasn't going to fire him? A bubble of hope rose in her chest. He'd be okay? If she was fired, would he be safe?

Tahlia shook her head, trying to clear it.

'Look, I'll let Mr Darrington explain why he's really here sitting in the Marketing Executive's chair, sorting through the personnel,' Raquel simpered, swinging around and heading out through the door. 'If you really need it spelt out to you…but you're an intelligent woman and, judging from your behaviour when I walked in, I'd say you know already, don't you think, Mr Darrington?'

What? She turned back to Case, who stood at the window, stiff like a tin soldier, his arms crossed tightly across his chest, his brow heavy.

The Rottie closed the office door.

Tahlia shook her head. 'Case, I feel there are a few things I need to say.'

'Likewise,' he said, his voice a monotone.

Tahlia sucked in a breath, a cold chill clawing at her belly. 'I have to say I was incredibly put out by your getting the position I'd coveted and I may have had ideas to rectify the situation, but that all changed.'

'I can imagine.'

'Case, look at me.'

He turned and faced her, his gaze steel-blue, his mouth pulled thin. 'And then you decided it was more in your interests to seduce me with your beautiful body, your sweet voice and your innocent damsel-in-distress act?'

'Yes. No. I didn't mean to,' she said softly. 'It wasn't an act.' How could he think that? She'd never enjoyed being with someone as much as she loved being with him, knowing him, loving him.

He shook his head. 'Not an act until you heard that the new owner *had already* put in the efficiency expert.'

Tahlia's blood chilled. Someone was already here going through the staff files? Who? Surely she'd have noticed, but she had been so busy focusing on her own problems, her loss, the frenzy of strange emotions she was having for her new boss.

She froze, ice seeping into her toes. 'You,' she said, her voice devoid of the emotion that rocked through her.

Oh, gawd. She was an idiot. Of course it was him!

He'd waltzed in, distracting everyone with his good looks and charm, diverting her attention to him and not to what he was doing.

She shook her head. What would he think of her? Raquel was right—she'd proved to him, one hundred and fifty per cent, that she was a fool.

Did he always test the staff this way? Sweep them off their feet and into warm arms that weren't safe at all, that weren't to be trusted, that weren't meant for her and for her alone.

Tahlia's eyes burned. She had been an idiot to think she was ready for a relationship...ever!

She blinked hard and lifted her gaze. The coldness in his eyes burned through her.

How could she have let herself love him?

'Of course, I knew that all along,' she blurted, her voice rough, hoping he'd believe the lie. 'You being so obviously out of your field of expertise, put in a position of power and yet…wanting to spend all your time trawling through personnel files. Not something a new executive would put first on his list, not what I'd do, and I figured you'd like games.'

'I should have guessed.' Case clenched his hands by his sides. 'It was a chance to ingratiate yourself and secure the position you coveted, I'm guessing.'

Tahlia nodded tightly. 'I knew exactly who you were from the start,' she forced out, every word gouging holes in her heart. She had to save some semblance of pride in all this. 'The rumour mill, you know.'

Case looked away. 'Right. Of course. So you knew that I could give you exactly what you wanted, if you played me right?'

She forced a smile to her mouth. 'Of course. I figured if I put together a file on you…I'd prove that I was executive material…and really was passionate about the job and…' the words were like bile '…then I figured why not guarantee my promotion—'

'Right, of course. You knew,' he said, his voice devoid of all emotion. 'I'd hoped I had a few weeks before the news of my purchase was heard here.'

His purchase? *He* was the owner? Tahlia stared blankly at him, the word ricocheting through her. He was the man behind the company that had bought WWW Designs? And he was here, pretending to be just anyone?

'A couple of weeks to get the job done,' Case said casually, '…and I…I usually…entertain myself on the job. Life can be so boring…and since you seemed more than keen to—'

Tahlia's chest ached, right down to her toes. He *was*

a class A playboy snob looking to entertain himself until something better came along and she'd been used. 'Glad to be of service, sir,' she bit out. 'Just doing my bit. For you…the office… Me.'

She backed away from the man who was a stranger to her. And she'd given him everything on a platter— the staff, her friends, her father, and her heart.

How could she have trusted him?

He turned to face her. 'Just wanted to let you know that I enjoyed the game. Thanks. I especially enjoyed the sincerity with which you shared all the pertinent information you wanted to get across about the staff. I'll take into account the tainted nature—and your possible ulterior motives—in that discourse when I make my decisions.'

Tahlia moved behind the chair and gripped the back, holding herself up on legs that wanted to fold underneath her. How stupid had she been to share all that with him? The enemy.

She stared at his handsome face, just made to woo women into madness, fighting the ache in her throat.

If only she could take back the last week and keep her distance, her cool, her fears and dreams to herself. 'I should imagine you would take everything I said with a grain of salt.'

She glanced at the door. 'So—' That was it then. There was nothing for it than to skulk back to her office and pack her desk, knowing that the first man she'd let in had not only stuck a knife deep in her career, but had also twisted it deep in her chest. And she only had herself to blame.

'So—' Case strode to his desk. 'You get the pro-

motion that you wanted, Marketing Executive. I think
you're just the sort of ruthless career-minded person
we want to have leading the charge.'

Tahlia shook her head, her vision blurring. She
couldn't have heard right. He was giving her the job
thinking that she was some manipulating ladder-
climber?

'You have the promotion, Miss Moran,' he said in a
monotone voice, not looking at her. 'You can start as
Marketing Executive on Monday.'

She lifted her chin. He was giving her the promotion
she'd wanted, the dream she'd coveted, and it felt so
very very wrong.

She didn't want to be a part of a business that em-
ployed the sort of person he thought she was.

She took a step backwards. She'd been an idiot to
open her heart, leave herself vulnerable, show her
weaknesses to him…to trust him.

'Great, thanks,' she shot out coldly. 'I'm so glad we
don't have to continue this farce—a bit much of an
effort, yeah?' She held herself tight. 'I appreciate it.'

He nodded tightly, a muscle in his jaw flicking.

'And I'm guessing I'll get the generous rise that goes
with the job,' she bit out. 'Seeing as I did such a good
job entertaining you and all, not that I didn't enjoy you
a bit.' Too much. Way too much. 'You were a great
change from the hulking suits that usually are in a position to give me a boost in my career.' She inched
backwards, her heart thundering protests. 'That I
couldn't possibly get on my own merits,' she forced
out, every word scouring her throat.

Case stood like a statue behind his large desk, staring

at her, his face grim. 'I have to say you were the smoothest operator, the best I've...the—'

She shrugged, heading for the door, dragging in a deep breath, blinking the moisture from her eyes. 'I'm surprised you didn't guess that a cutthroat career woman like myself would be dying for that chair, would do anything.'

A shadow passed over his face. 'Yes, I should have,' he said, his voice deep and husky.

Tahlia paused at the door, her throat aching with screams. 'What prompted you to come in yourself, by the way, rather than send someone else?'

'I was bored.' Case shrugged and sat down in the leather chair. 'Thanks for breaking the monotony. And, since I've given you the promotion, I'd appreciate you continuing to keep the fact that I'm the new owner to yourself.'

'Glad to do my bit,' she said strongly. 'But how do you know that I haven't told everyone already?'

'Believe me, I'd know. I can recognise flattery and posing a mile off.' He gave her a cold, hard look, as though looking at her for the first time.

'Right, okay, then. I'll go then and leave you to decide the fate of the rest of the office without me distracting you with my games,' she said in a rush.

'Appreciated,' Case said, shuffling the papers on his desk. 'Goodbye, Miss Moran.'

'Goodbye,' she whispered, her voice failing her. She strode through the door and down the hall. She should have stuck to her rules, her list, to business and not personal.

She had been right to avoid a personal life. She

didn't need it or to have her heart ripped out and crushed.

She touched her lips and her vision blurred. She'd never kiss his lying mouth, hold his playboy body close, hear his traitorous heart again...

How could she have been so stupid? She should have known he'd let her down, betray her trust, believe what he wanted to believe and do what he wanted. He was just like her father.

Tahlia stopped at the desk and pulled out her hand-bag and shoved her favourite pens, a stapler and a few rubber bands in. At least she had her promotion.

The thought made her feel ill; as if she'd take any-thing she hadn't earned. This was all so wrong. It wasn't meant to be like this.

He was meant to be wonderful. He was meant to be the one. He was meant to be her perfect partner who was there to support her, not break her heart into little pieces.

Tahlia fought against the chill in her veins.

She hooked her bag on her shoulder and strode down the hall. She'd email a resignation. She couldn't ever see the lying jerk again.

Although there was one more thing to give him before she left.

TO: *allstaff@WWWDesigns.com*
FROM: *TahliaM@WWWDesigns.com*
RE: WWW Designs' newest employee
Please be advised that Case *Trustless* Darrington is in fact the new owner of WWW Designs and is in the process of making staff evaluations.

All those interested in keeping their jobs, please note
Mr Darrington is currently using the Marketing
Executive office, where all reports, visitors and any
gifts, donations and flattery will be gratefully re-
ceived. (NB: he has a sweet tooth)
Thanks to you all for making my work days satis-
fying and special. My thoughts and good wishes are
with you all.
Tahlia Moran
Ex-Director of Sales

CHAPTER EIGHTEEN

Sagittarians—Think before you make big decisions.

CASE still heard the door shutting after Tahlia left yesterday, haunting him with its finality. He hadn't watched her leave, couldn't bear to see her or let *her* see the pain in his eyes, the crushing weight on his chest.

His worst nightmare had come true and the sequel hurt far more than the original ever had—how could that be?

Dammit. How had he let her under his radar? When he had known she was trouble from the first moment he'd laid eyes on her.

Hadn't he learnt anything with Celia?

How could he have believed that he'd get it right by being naïve and stupid like last time? He should have investigated her and known more about her than she knew herself. Then he wouldn't have to feel this way.

Tahlia's confession had said it all. She was a player. She hadn't even denied it. Had revelled in it. Had yanked out his heart and crushed it under her sharp truths, shattering what he'd held so dear, so close, so incredibly beautiful to him that morning, with the dream of spending for ever with her. Of her having his children, of sharing his heart, his dreams, his life.

He pulled at his tie. He had been a fool. Again.

When was he going to learn not to give in to the optimistic organ in his chest and rely on his head?

He couldn't even fire her. He should have, but if that job was what she really wanted then he had to give it to her…if that was all he could ever give her.

Case raked his hands through his hair, glancing at his watch. Time to play the executive again. Hell. Could he pull it off now, with Tahlia's game playing over and over in his head, trying to put together the skewed logic she'd had in playing him.

Why had she bothered when she'd known who he was from the start? All she had had to do was be competent and efficient and she'd have had her precious promotion…

He rubbed his face; he couldn't make her out. He'd spent all night tossing, trying to fit the woman he knew she was to the one she had said she was.

Nothing made sense.

A knock on the door tore him from his thoughts. Was it her? Had she changed her mind and decided she wanted to share a bit more with him before he left, that he wasn't so abhorrent and she could stand his company even when it didn't serve a means to an end?

'Come,' he barked, his voice hoarse.

Chrystal poked her head around the corner. 'Is it safe to come in?'

'Yes,' he said with a sigh. 'But leave the door open.'

'I'm here to help,' she said smoothly, striding into the room, her hips swaying in her knee-length tweed skirt.

'Help?' He put a pile of papers between him and the

woman in front of him, feeling some comfort in her demure outfit but not in the look in her eyes.

'Yes. I'm here as a shoulder to cry on, or an ear to listen to your angst, or to answer whatever questions you have about the office.'

'Cry? Angst?' He straightened in his chair. Was he that obvious? He hoped not. There was no way he wanted Tahlia to know how much she'd meant to him. 'Would you please explain yourself?'

She plucked out a plate of cookies from behind her back. 'These are for you. And just in case you don't remember, I'm Chrystal from Reception, the one who'd love to have a chance to mend your broken heart.'

'Right.' He waved a hand. 'Thank you so much but I have to be honest and tell you there's no chance for you and I at all. I'd be doing you a disservice if I led you to believe otherwise. I'm not attracted to you at all.'

Chrystal leant heavily on the desk, leaning over towards him. 'Okay, if you're sure. And, just so you know, it's so nice to work with someone as clever, handsome and incredibly intelligent as you.'

Case tugged at his tie. 'Thank you.'

A tap at the door jerked him from the gleam in the woman's eyes. A pretty woman with dark hair stood at the door, her hand resting on the bulge of her pregnancy. 'Is this a good time?'

'Absolutely,' Case said quickly, standing up. 'Thank you, Chrystal.' He watched Chrystal leave, every step she took a relief to the tension in his shoulders and neck. 'What can I do for you, Miss…Rhodes, Mrs Brant or—?'

'Keely is fine.' The young woman moved into the office. 'Just thought I'd drop in some doughnuts,' she said, sweeping out a box of iced doughnuts from behind her back and putting it down on his desk. 'And to find out if you could tell me what's going on with Tahlia.'

Case swallowed hard. 'Miss Moran. Yes. She's a very strong-willed young woman who obviously knows what she wants and has no hesitation in going after it.'

Keely nodded, her eyes narrowed. She tilted her head, opened her mouth, then closed it. 'That she is,' she said. 'We'll all miss her.'

Miss her? As Director of Sales, he guessed. Despite her ruthlessness, she did seem to have a warm rapport with the staff.

'Just a minute, Miss…Mrs…Keely. One question.'

She glared at him. 'Yes, Mr Darrington?'

'Is Tahlia…Miss Moran…afraid of heights?'

'Is grass green? Absolutely. She's terrified. Has been since…' She trailed off.

He clenched his hands. That at least had been real. 'Her father died,' he murmured.

Keely's brow furrowed. 'She told *you* that?'

Case's gut tightened.

'She doesn't tell anybody that.' Keely swung around and waddled back to the doorway, weaving her way through a crowd of employees milling in the hallway, all brandishing plates, bags, bows and flowers.

What in hell was going on?

He punched the computer he'd ignored all morning in favour of staring morosely at Tahlia's file.

Case stabbed his computer keys, logging on.

TO: *CaseD@WWWDesigns.com*
FROM: *TahliaM@WWWDesigns.com*
SUBJECT: Resignation.

Please be advised that I, Tahlia Moran, hereby give my notice to my smart-arsed sexy-as-hell boss who I wouldn't want to work for because he didn't fire me for unethical behaviour.

I'd like it noted that I will not be returning to WWW Designs, due to the accrued sick leave and the holidays that I didn't take due to my commitment above-and-beyond to the company.

Please note that I am a professional, Mr Darrington, and hope that both my dalliance with you and my impromptu absence has not put you to any convenience.

Tahlia Moran

Case jerked to his feet, a hot warmth spreading through him. She didn't want the job!

Oh, hell. Could this mean what every inch of him wanted it to? Or was this another chapter in her game?

Was she for real?

Could he slap his heart back in his chest one last time and take a chance?

He pushed back his chair, replaying that moment in his office, knowing the job didn't matter...

Oh, hell, he'd made the biggest mistake of his life.

CHAPTER NINETEEN

Dear Diary,
Some idiot said it was better to have loved and lost
than never have loved at all—load of crap. If I didn't
know love, I would never know this pain or care about
an arrogant jerk that didn't deserve anything,
least of all my love.

TO: *Tahlia007@hotmail.com.au*
CC: *KeelyR@WWWDesigns.com*
FROM: *EmmaR@WWWDesigns.com*
RE: Case Darrington

I can't believe you're resigning. Not possible.
Whatever happened? And Case is the owner? How
did you find out? What happened with you two? You
looked so happy.

I saw Case today. He doesn't look happy, although
all the gifts that are flooding in should at least satisfy
that sweet tooth.

Hope you're going to be there for the baby shower.
Do you need soup? Company? Chocolate?

Just found out. Chrystal is after Case. Saw her gush-
ing all over him. And for the office playboy you
thought he was, he wasn't looking all that thrilled
about the attention.

Why aren't you answering my calls?

Em

Tahlia chewed on the end of her pen, staring at her home desktop, stabbing the computer keyboard. Served him right to have Chrystal after him.

> TO: *Tahlia007@hotmail.com*
> CC: *EmmaR@WWWDesigns.com*
> FROM: *KeelyR@WWWDesigns.com*
> RE: Case Darrington
> Just heard Liam asked Chrystal out! And she said yes, as long as he understood she wasn't going to have sex with him. So, virgin still she may be, reluctant to be blunt, no way.
> Liam is head over heels. Hope Chrystal realises how nice he is and doesn't break his heart.
> How's your heart, Tahlia?
> K

Tahlia pushed away from the desk she had in the corner of her room, hauling herself out of the chair and weaving her way through the books that couldn't take her mind off him, clothes that didn't feel right on her skin and take-away boxes on the floor.

She'd binged all yesterday, had tried to smother the ache in her belly with pizza, Chinese, doughnuts, ice cream and chocolate, to no avail.

She'd spent the morning in bed with the phone off the hook. She couldn't face talking to anyone, let alone her mother.

How could her mother tempt fate and trust a man again? The thought made her stomach toss... It was just a matter of time before she was hurt again.

How could she be such a fool?

Tahlia slapped her cheeks. She had to shape up. She couldn't miss Keely's baby shower, no matter what she felt.

Tahlia pushed open her bedroom door. She ought to find something to wear, have a shower, drag her sorry-arse out and pretend to be happy.

At least she could be happy that her two best friends had found love, and even Chrystal. Fancy that it was Case that Chrystal was keen on, who she'd done the incredible makeover thing for, who she'd reclaimed her virgin status to entice.

Tahlia kicked yesterday's clothes out of her way and stopped. That meant that Chrystal's guy, the one who was still getting over the wounds of a really nasty divorce, was Case. Great.

What did the man do? Deliberately torture unwitting females into falling madly in love with him and sacrificing everything for him so he could get some revenge on the species for his pain?

She swiped at her cheeks, damp again. She wouldn't put it past him. Rich, lying, manipulating snob that he was.

How could he be that guy?

She shook herself. It didn't matter anyway. She knew what he thought of her and he'd shown her just how much love could hurt, and she didn't want it.

She was better off with a glass-chewing bartender covered in tattoos.

The doorbell rang. She glanced at her watch. Probably Em or Keely. She'd pretended to be out, hiding deeper under her blankets when they'd come by last night.

She knew she couldn't avoid them for long, especially when she was expected at the baby shower tonight.

Tahlia traipsed to the door, straightening her T-shirt over her jogging bottoms, and trying to comb her loose hair with her fingers.

She pulled open the door.

Case *Traitor* Darrington stood in her doorway, almost filling it, his dark suit sitting perfectly on his body, his hair ruffled, his jaw slightly shadowed.

He cast a glance over her as though drinking in the sight of her. 'Hey.'

'Hey,' she echoed, willing herself to slam the door closed in his handsome face so she didn't have to hear what mean thing he was going to reveal to her next, but she was frozen.

'I came over to find out why you resigned when I gave you the promotion you were desperate for. And also why everyone is bringing me sweets.'

She tried to smile. 'Oh. Haven't you read the email?'

Case nodded. 'You spilled the beans, then, which I find incredibly odd seeing how hard you worked for the promotion.'

She shrugged. She couldn't do this. She wasn't up to this. 'The beans are spilt. The news is out. I've resigned. Let's leave it at that, okay?' She tried to close the door.

Case put his hand up, holding the door. 'Not okay. I think we have a few things to discuss.'

Tahlia swung the door wide and retreated to the lounge, throwing herself into her favourite chair, tucking up her legs and staring at her fish, who were swimming around the bowl as though nothing was wrong at all. 'Fine. What?'

Case closed the front door behind him and leant against the wall. 'Tell me why you resigned.'

'I told you, I didn't want to work for a place that would hire me even after what I'd done.'

'Really?'

'Would you? If the boss saw you as a manipulative career-climbing user,' she blurted, holding herself tightly, swallowing the burning ache in her throat.

He strode to her chair and squatted, holding the arms to steady himself. 'Tell me why you'd go to all that trouble finding out all my flaws as a Marketing Executive if you knew who I was from the start.'

She glanced at the man with the sapphire-blue eyes who had torn her heart in half. How could she trust him again? She knew what trusting a man got you. Pain.

'Please, Tahlia, tell me.'

Tahlia lifted her chin and looked at the man and knew deep in her heart that this was her chance to move on. To open herself and tell him like it was, not because he deserved to hear it, not because her mother said so, not because it was a good career move, but for her and her alone. It was time to let the past go and make her own future, and all her own mistakes.

'I didn't. I didn't know who you were,' she blurted, her eyes stinging. 'When I bumped into you in the foyer I felt things I didn't want to feel. When you took my promotion I decided to smother those feelings with anger. When there was no anger left I covered those feelings with all the reasons you shouldn't have got my job.' She sucked in a deep breath, fighting the ache in her throat. 'And when I found out how nice you were I gave into them, for you.'

'Tahlia.' Case sighed. 'And when did you find out who I was?'

She looked away, her cheeks heating at her stupidity and ignorance of his role at WWW. 'When *you* told me.'

His brow furrowed. 'Then—?'

'I'm not that person,' she whispered, 'that you think I am. I can't be. I earn my own way, through hard work, intelligence and commitment, not—' She glanced at the bedroom door.

'Hell, Tahlia.' Case dropped to his knees on the floor in front of her. 'I'm so sorry. I've been the biggest jerk. When I heard that you were only interested in your career—what you could get out of me—everything that went wrong in my marriage came back to haunt me.'

She stared into his face. 'It's okay. I'm fine. I'll be fine. There's plenty more jobs around.' She lifted her chin defiantly.

'Tahlia, I need to explain.'

'What's to explain?' She shrugged. 'You just lied about everything.'

'I was there to do a job.'

She nodded tightly.

'The job is all I've ever had to hang on to when my life wasn't working, all the more so in the last few years. I've been so burnt in the past I wasn't willing to let myself have a future. I wanted you to like me for me, not because of what I owned.'

'I don't care what you own.'

'What do you care about?'

Tahlia stared at the man she loved so much it hurt. 'I did want that promotion and I did want to prove to Raquel she'd made a mistake in hiring you instead of me.'

'I would have done the same.'

Tahlia leant forward, cupping his face in her hands. 'I had to spend time with you to prove my point…but then I realised I wanted your kisses, your touch, the magic you offered, just for me. All me.' She bit her lip. 'And I wanted more.'

'The job?'

She shook her head slowly, her gaze glued to his. 'You. I wanted to keep you.'

Case's eyes brightened. 'Why?'

Tahlia stared at her hands in her lap. She knew it was time. She had to say it out loud. Sure, she had no control over what his reaction would be, what would happen next, but she owed this to herself. 'Because I love you, Case T Darrington.'

Case touched her chin with his finger, lifting her gaze to meet his. 'Hell, Tahlia, I've never met anyone like you.'

'And that's good?'

'Of course it is.' He drew her into his arms, brushing his lips against hers. 'I love you too, with all my heart and soul. Can you forgive me for being an idiot?'

'I think I can.' Tahlia couldn't help but smile. Sure, there were going to be risks in loving someone else but she couldn't imagine living a day without Case in it. 'By the way, what does the T stand for in your name?'

Case wrapped her in his warm, strong arms and held

her close, swamped by the incredible turn in his life. He'd learned all right, how to love, and he would never let anything be more important, ever.

'My middle name,' he murmured, pulling her closer and breathing in her sweet scent. 'Trustworthy.'

EPILOGUE

They say that love's what makes the world
go round. I say keep me spinning.

EMMA strode back to Keely's lounge chair and dropped on to Harry's knee, pulling a stuffed giraffe on to her lap and an arm around her fiancé. 'Phew. That was the last guest.'

Tahlia scooped the rest of the mountain of wrapping paper into a rubbish bag, surveying the pile of presents on the coffee table—baby rugs, bouncers, bottles, nappies and teddies galore. 'You've got everything you need now, Keely.'

Keely smiled, snuggling into Lachlan's arms, cradling her big belly with both her hands. 'I sure have. And you know what, I think you guys do too.'

Tahlia glanced to Emma, who was caressing Harry's face with the giraffe, her eyes shining.

'I do,' Em piped, tossing the giraffe behind the sofa and using her lips instead.

'I can't believe you'll be saying "I do" in a couple of weeks,' Tahlia offered softly. 'In front of your family and your friends.'

Emma laughed. 'I can't wait.'

Tahlia turned to the amazing man behind her, the man who had touched her life in so many ways, the

183

man *she* was taking to the wedding. She moved closer to where he sat in the chair.

Case leant over, brushing his lips over her cheek. 'I like your friends,' he whispered, his breath hot on her skin. 'And I love you.'

Tahlia stood up, the warmth of his words filling her, glancing around at the wonderful people who were her colleagues, her friends, her family. She loved them all, needed them all, wanted them all to stay in her life, but one in particular…

She looked down at Case, his eyes shining with his love for her.

'Hey,' Keely said. 'Six months ago did any of us think we would be *here*?'

'Nope.' Em laughed. 'Not a chance.'

'No way,' Tahlia said, dropping into Case's strong, safe arms, her heart full of love she'd never thought could be hers. 'But there's no place I'd rather be.'

TO: *TahliaM@WWWDesigns.com*
CC: *KeelyR@WWWDesigns.com*
FROM: *EmmaR@WWWDesigns.com*
RE: Love and promotions

Saw Liam and Chrystal down at Sammy's, all over each other—it was so beautiful.

Can't wait to receive my orders from my very own best friend, the new Marketing Executive, Tahlia Moran, woman in love.

Can't believe you didn't accept the position of General Manager—yippee, the wicked Rottie is gone—although I have to admire your dedication to working your way to the top on your own merits.

How's Case going? Is he getting a work-out? Does he like your merits? And is that a ring on your finger? Tell all.
Em

MILLS & BOON®

Live the emotion

Tender romance™

A MOST SUITABLE WIFE *by Jessica Steele*

Taye Trafford needs someone to share her flat – and the bills – fast! So, when Magnus Ashthorpe turns up, Taye offers him the room, not knowing he actually has an entirely different reason for living there: because he believes Taye is the mistress who has caused his sister's heartbreak!

IN THE ARMS OF THE SHEIKH *by Sophie Weston*

Natasha Lambert is horrified by what she must wear as her best friend's bridesmaid! Worse, the best man is Kazim al Saraq – an infuriatingly charming sheikh with a dazzling wit and an old-fashioned take on romance. He's determined to win Natasha's heart – and she's terrified he might succeed...!

THE MARRIAGE MIRACLE *by Liz Fielding*

An accident three years ago has left Matilda Lang in a wheelchair, and hotshot New York banker Sebastian Wolseley is the man who can make – or break – her heart. It would take a miracle for Matty to risk her heart after what she's been through, but Sebastian knows he can help her...

ORDINARY GIRL, SOCIETY GROOM
by Natasha Oakley

Eloise Lawson has finally found the family she's never known. But, cast adrift in their high society world, she can only depend on one person: broodingly handsome Jeremy Norland. But if she falls in love with him she could lose everything. Will Eloise have the courage to risk all?

On sale 2nd December 2005

Available at most branches of WHSmith, Tesco, ASDA, Borders, Eason, Sainsbury's and most bookshops

Visit www.millsandboon.co.uk

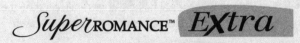

Make your Christmas wish list – and check it twice! ★

Watch out for these very special holiday stories – all featuring the incomparable charm and romance of the Christmas season.

By Jasmine Cresswell, Tara Taylor
Quinn and Kate Hoffmann
On sale 21st October 2005

By Lynnette Kent and
Sherry Lewis
On sale 21st October 2005

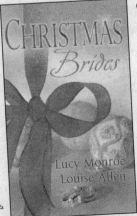

By Lucy Monroe and
Louise Allen
On sale 4th November 2005

1105/XMAS/LIST 2a

**By Heather Graham,
Lindsay McKenna, Marilyn
Pappano and Annette Broadrick**
On sale 18th November 2005

**By Marion Lennox, Josie Metcalfe
and Kate Hardy**
On sale 2nd December 2005

**By Margaret Moore, Terri Brisbin
and Gail Ranstrom**
On sale 2nd December 2005

**By Lisa Jackson, Barbara Boswell
and Linda Turner**
On sale 18th November 2005

1105/XMAS/LIST 2a

Celebrate Christmas with the Fortunes!

Enjoy three classic stories with the Fortunes—a family whose Christmas legacy is greater than mere riches.

ANGEL BABY by Lisa Jackson
Lesley Bastian is so grateful to Chase Fortune for delivering her baby – but trying to penetrate the walls around Chase's heart is almost as challenging as motherhood!

A HOME FOR CHRISTMAS by Barbara Boswell
As CEO of a major corporation, Ryder Fortune has little time for romance – until his assistant Joanna Chandler works her way into his hardened heart…

THE CHRISTMAS CHILD by Linda Turner
Naomi Windsong's little girl is missing and only Hunter Fortune can find her. But will time prove to be Hunter's greatest enemy – and love his greatest challenge?

THE FORTUNES
The price of privilege—the power of family.

On sale 18th November 2005

FREE

4 BOOKS AND A SURPRISE GIFT!

We would like to take this opportunity to thank you for reading this Mills & Boon® book by offering you the chance to take FOUR more specially selected titles from the Tender Romance™ series absolutely FREE! We're also making this offer to introduce you to the benefits of the Reader Service™—

- ★ **FREE home delivery**
- ★ **FREE gifts and competitions**
- ★ **FREE monthly Newsletter**
- ★ **Books available before they're in the shops**
- ★ **Exclusive Reader Service offers**

Accepting these FREE books and gift places you under no obligation to buy; you may cancel at any time, even after receiving your free shipment. Simply complete your details below and return the entire page to the address below. You don't even need a stamp!

YES! Please send me 4 free Tender Romance books and a surprise gift. I understand that unless you hear from me, I will receive 6 superb new titles every month for just £2.75 each, postage and packing free. I am under no obligation to purchase any books and may cancel my subscription at any time. The free books and gift will be mine to keep in any case.

N5ZEE

Ms/Mrs/Miss/Mr...Initials ....
BLOCK CAPITALS PLEASE

Surname ....

Address ....

....

....Postcode ....

Send this whole page to:
The Reader Service, FREEPOST CN81, Croydon, CR9 3WZ